Dear parents, caregivers, and educators:

If you want to get your child excited about reading, you've come to the right place! Ready-to-Read *GRAPHICS* is the perfect launchpad for emerging graphic novel readers.

All Ready-to-Read *GRAPHICS* books include the following:

- ★ **A how-to guide to reading graphic novels for first-time readers**

- ★ **Easy-to-follow panels to support reading comprehension**

- ★ **Accessible vocabulary to build your child's reading confidence**

- ★ **Compelling stories that star your child's favorite characters**

- ★ **Fresh, engaging illustrations that provide context and promote visual literacy**

Wherever your child may be on their reading journey, Ready-to-Read *GRAPHICS* will make them giggle, gasp, and want to keep reading more.

Blast off on this starry adventure . . . a universe of graphic novel reading awaits!

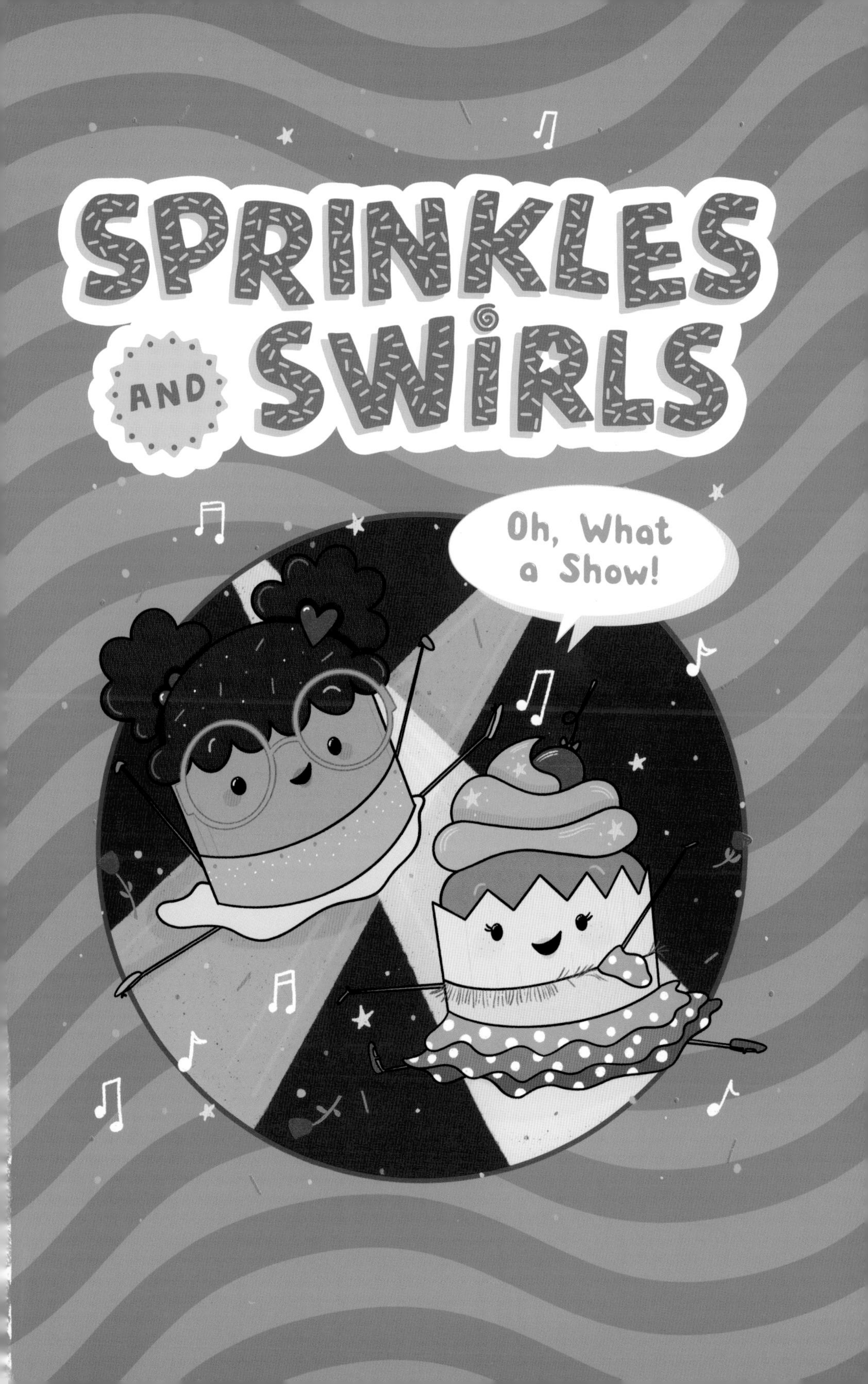
SPRINKLES
AND
SWIRLS
Oh, What a Show!

For sweet Octavia —L. S.

Dedicated to Emilia and Anina who are always ready for a good talent show! —S. A.

SIMON SPOTLIGHT

An imprint of Simon & Schuster Children's Publishing Division
1230 Avenue of the Americas, New York, New York 10020
This Simon Spotlight edition September 2022
Text copyright © 2022 by Lola M. Schaefer
Illustrations copyright © 2022 by Savannah Allen
All rights reserved, including the right of reproduction in whole or in part in any form.
SIMON SPOTLIGHT, READY-TO-READ, and colophon are registered trademarks of
Simon & Schuster, Inc.
For information about special discounts for bulk purchases, please contact Simon & Schuster Special
Sales at 1-866-506-1949 or business@simonandschuster.com.
Manufactured in China 0522 SCP
2 4 6 8 10 9 7 5 3 1
Library of Congress Cataloging-in-Publication Data
Names: Schaefer, Lola M., 1950- author. | Allen, Savannah, illustrator. Title: Oh, what a show! /
by Lola M. Schaefer ; illustrated by Savannah Allen. Description: Simon Spotlight edition. |
New York : Simon Spotlight, 2022. | Series: Sprinkles and Swirls | Audience: Ages 4-6. | Audience:
Grades K-1. | Summary: Cupcakes Sprinkles and Swirls decide to perform in the talent show, but first
need to decide what talent they want to showcase. Identifiers: LCCN 2021053464 (print) |
LCCN 2021053465 (ebook) | ISBN 9781665917957 (hardcover) | ISBN 9781665917964 (paperback) |
ISBN 9781665917971 (ebook) Subjects: CYAC: Graphic novels. | Cupcakes—Fiction. |
Talent shows—Fiction. | LCGFT: Graphic novels. Classification: LCC PZ7.7.S246 Oh 2022 (print)
| LCC PZ7.7.S246 (ebook) |DDC 741.5/973—dc23
LC record available at https://lccn.loc.gov/2021053464
LC ebook record available at https://lccn.loc.gov/2021053465

SPRINKLES AND SWIRLS

Oh, What a Show!

Written by **LOLA M. SCHAEFER** ✳ Illustrated by **SAVANNAH ALLEN**

Ready-to-Read *GRAPHICS*

Simon Spotlight
New York London Toronto Sydney New Delhi

HOW TO READ THIS BOOK

Sprinkles and Swirls are here to give you some tips on reading this book.

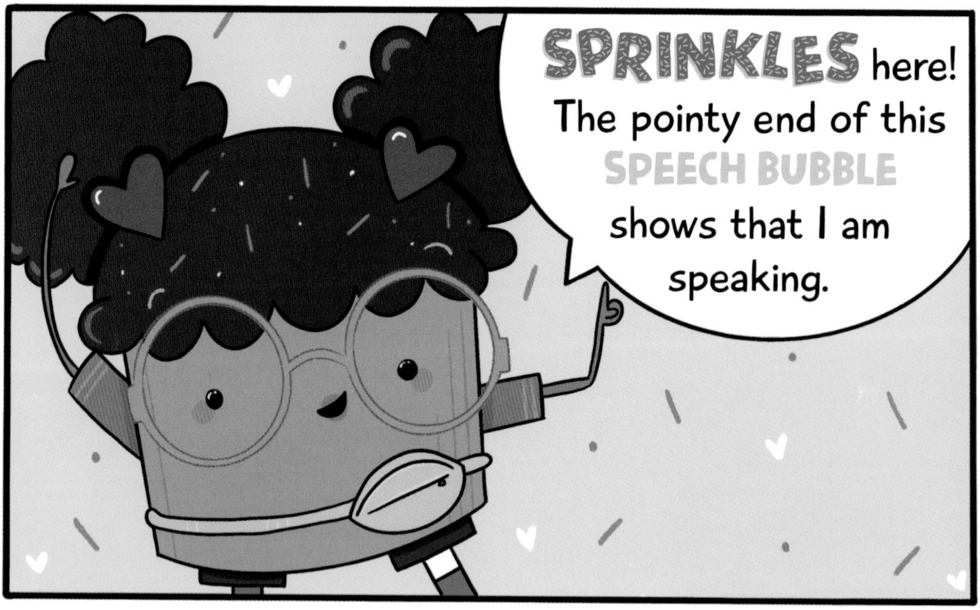
SPRINKLES here! The pointy end of this SPEECH BUBBLE shows that I am speaking.

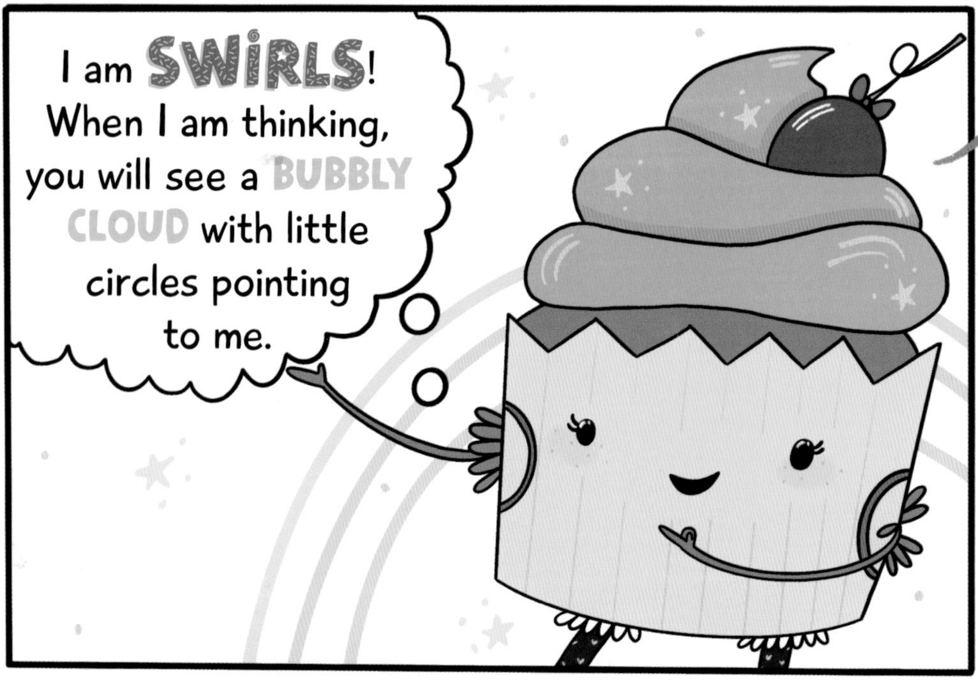
I am SWIRLS! When I am thinking, you will see a BUBBLY CLOUD with little circles pointing to me.

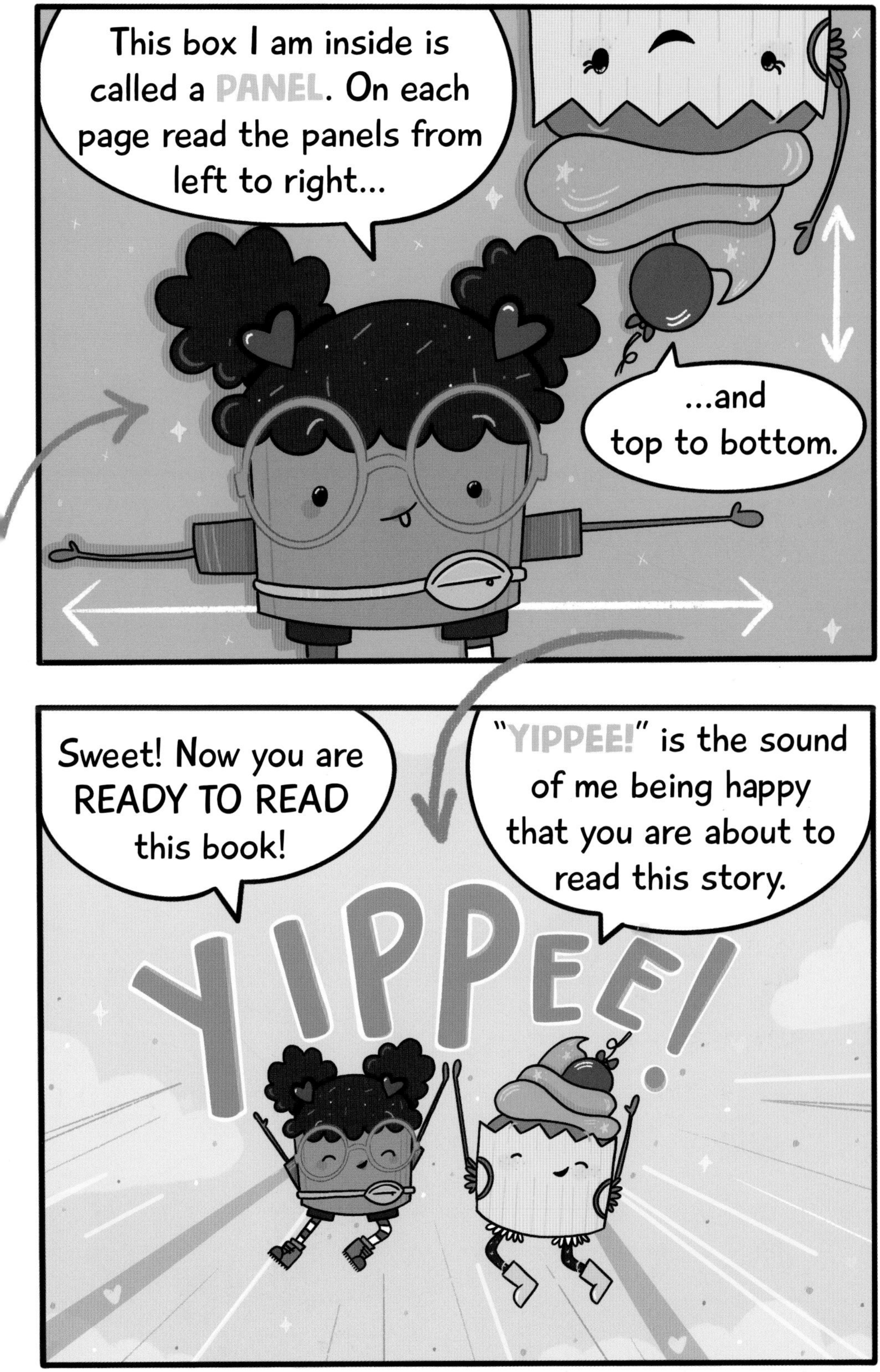
This box I am inside is called a PANEL. On each page read the panels from left to right...
...and top to bottom.
Sweet! Now you are READY TO READ this book!
"YIPPEE!" is the sound of me being happy that you are about to read this story.
YIPPEE!

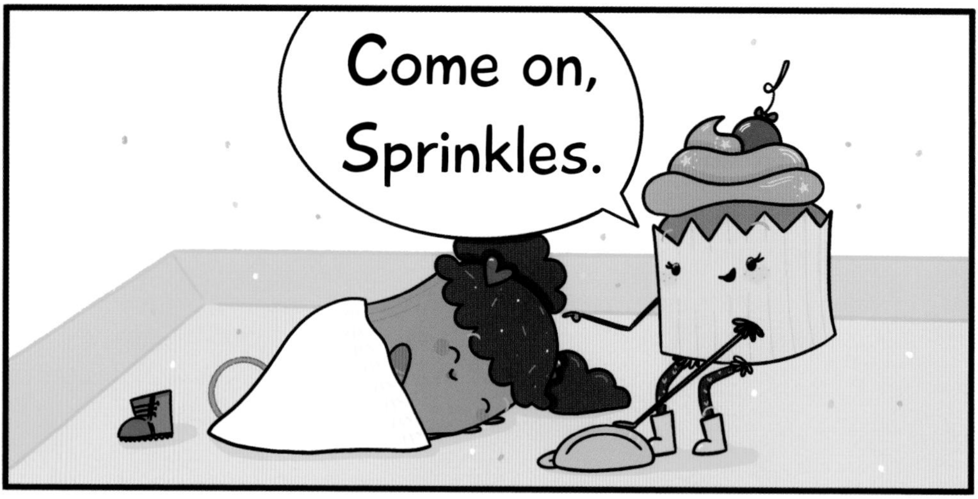
Come on, Sprinkles.

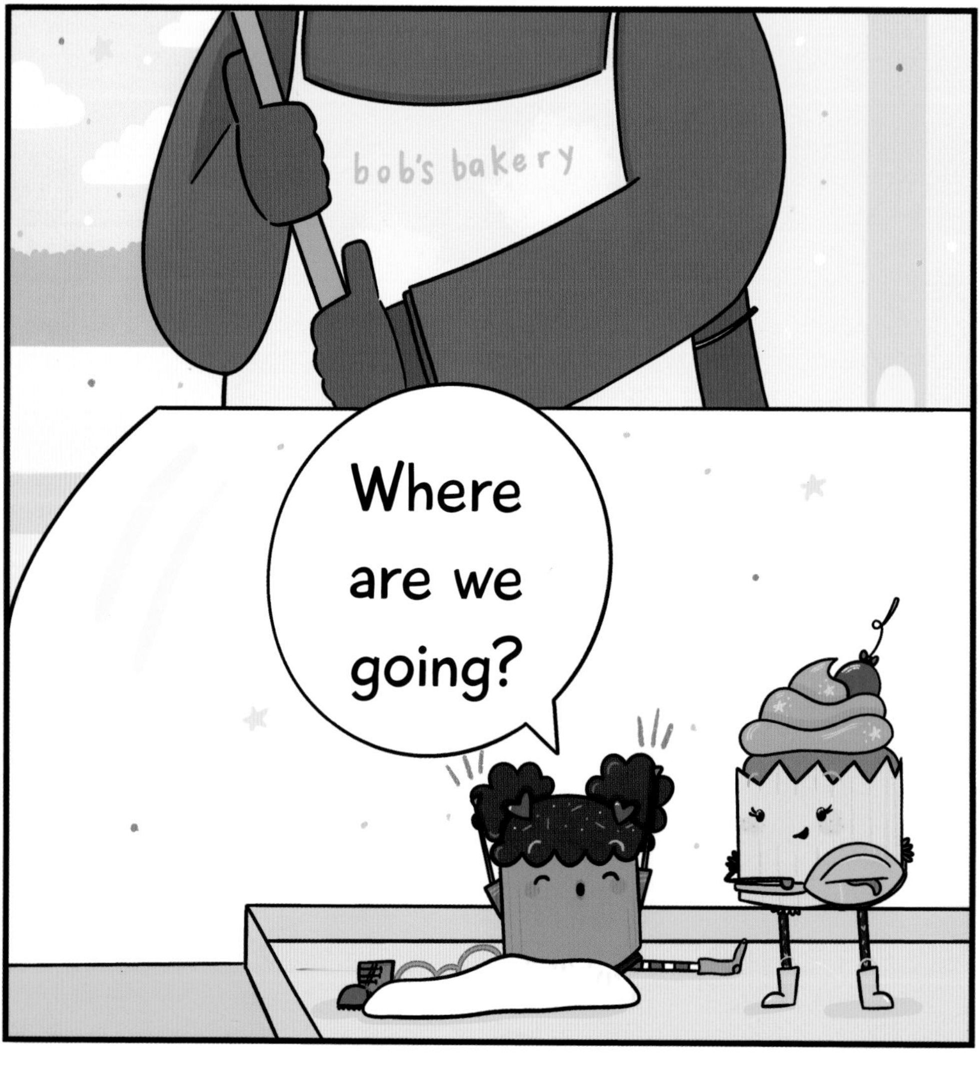
bob's bakery
Where are we going?

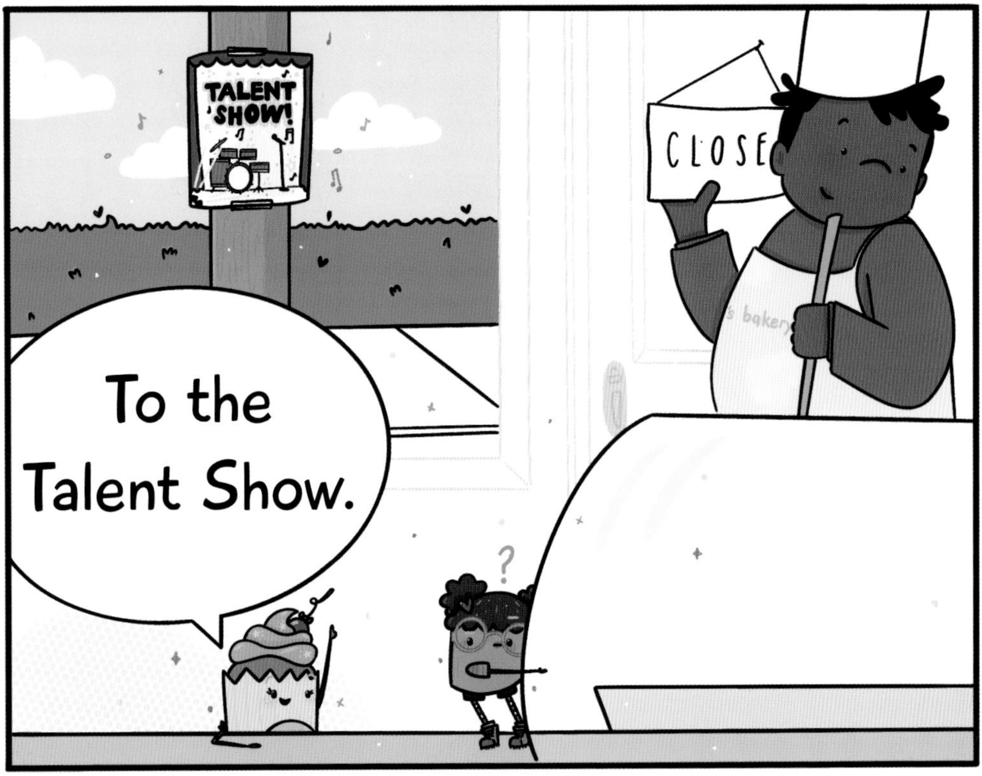
TALENT SHOW!
CLOSE
To the Talent Show.

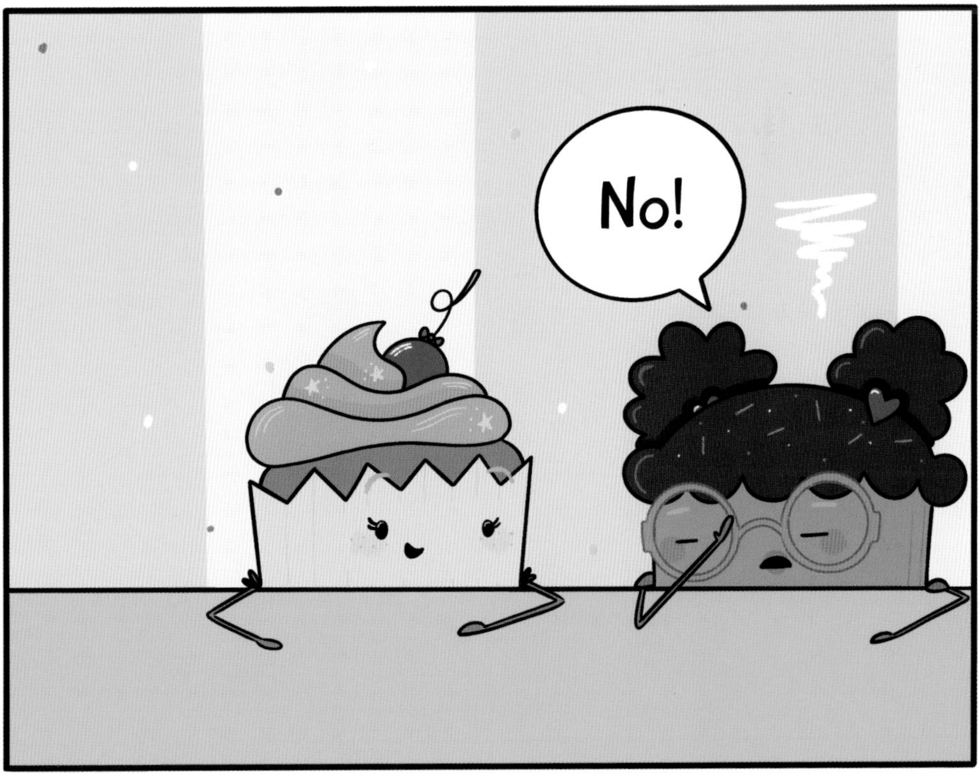
No!

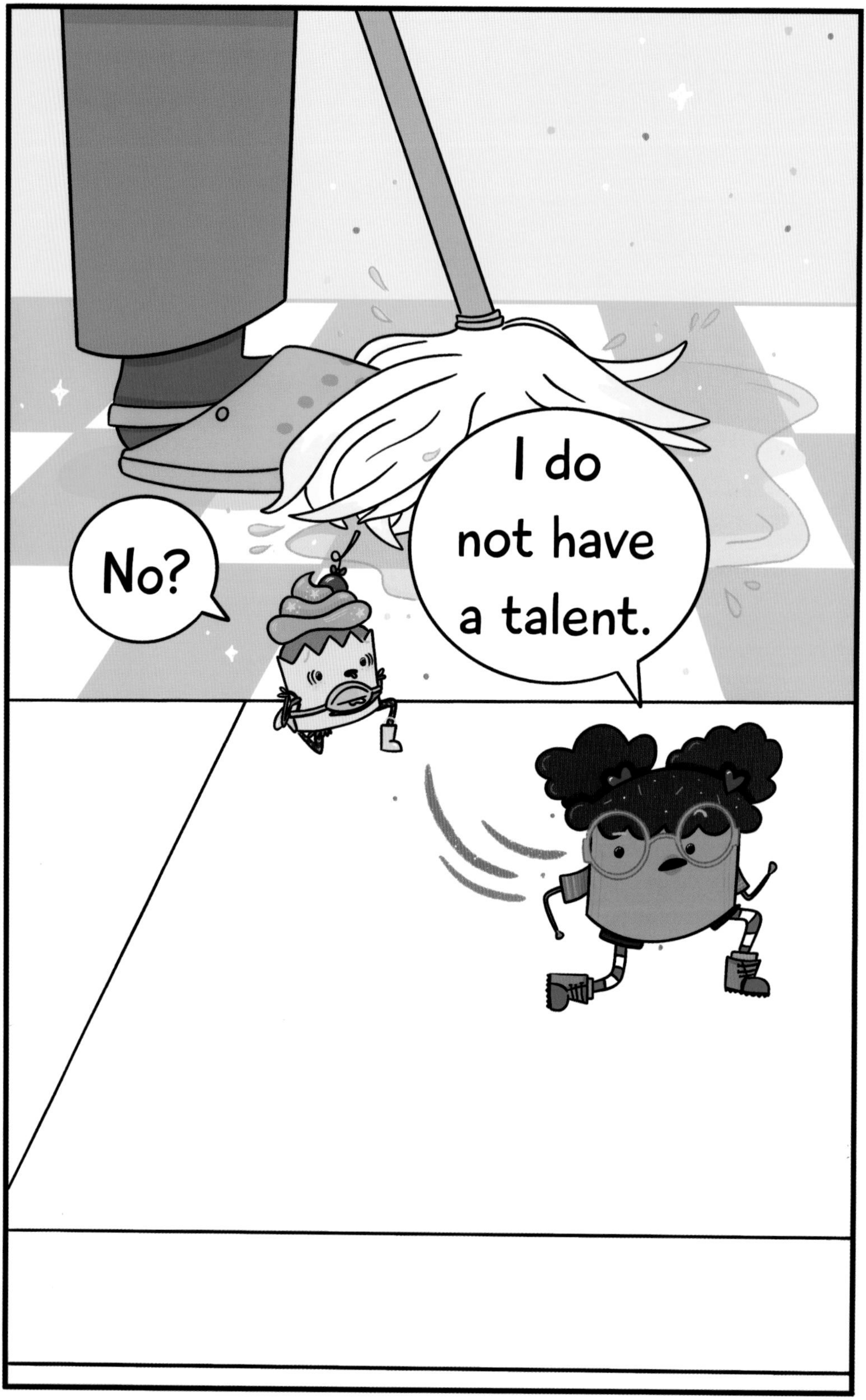
No?
I do not have a talent.

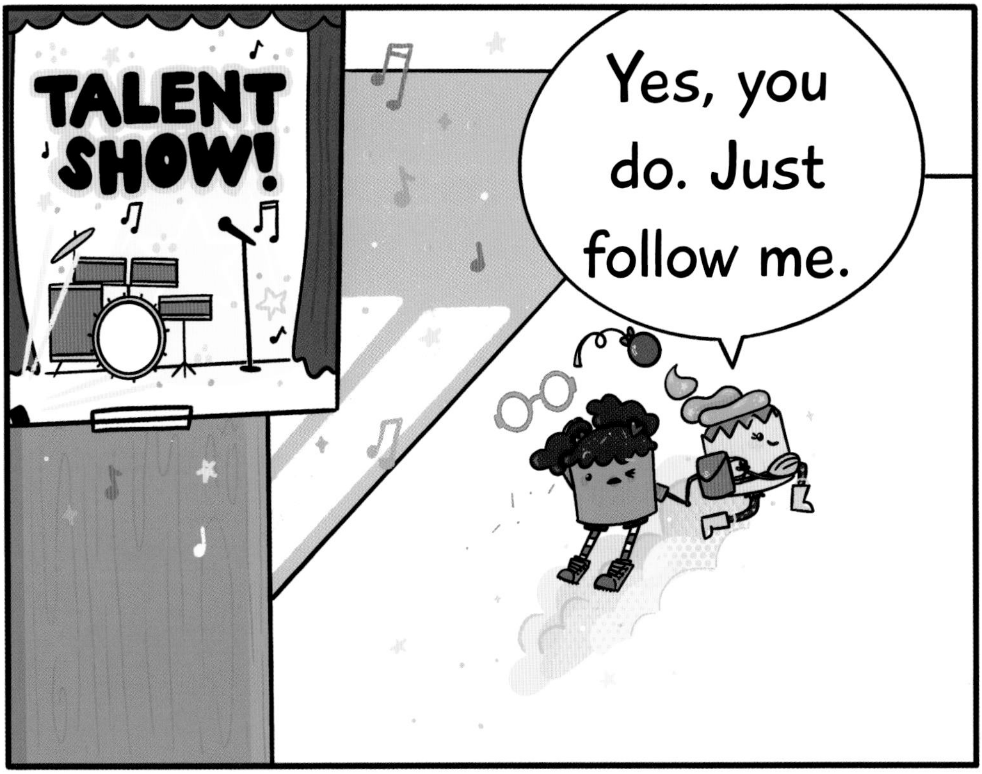
TALENT SHOW!
Yes, you do. Just follow me.

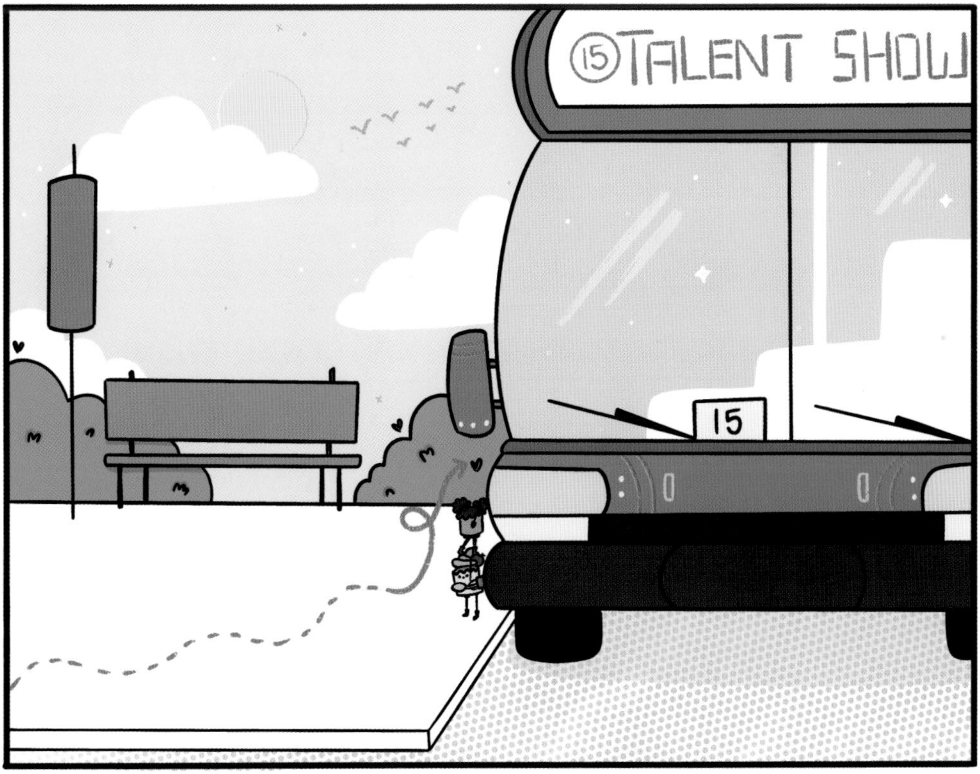
15 TALENT SHOW
15

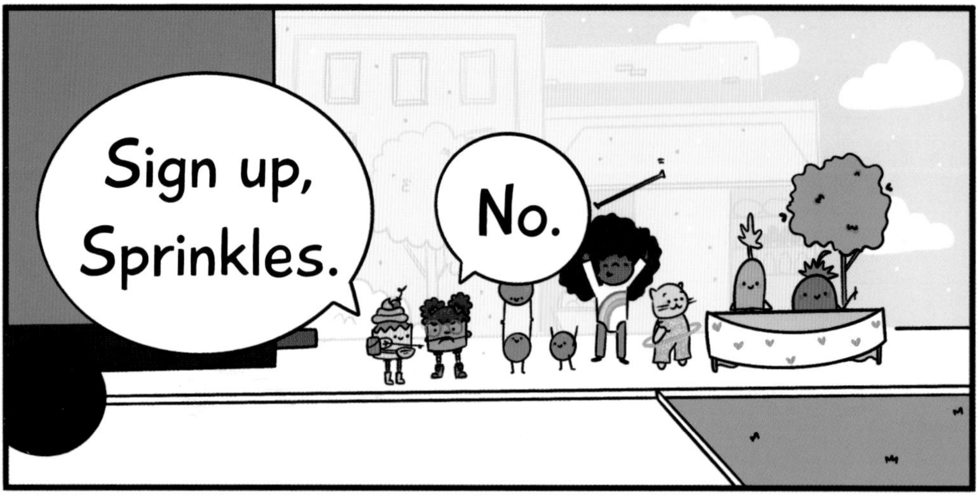
Sign up, Sprinkles.
No.

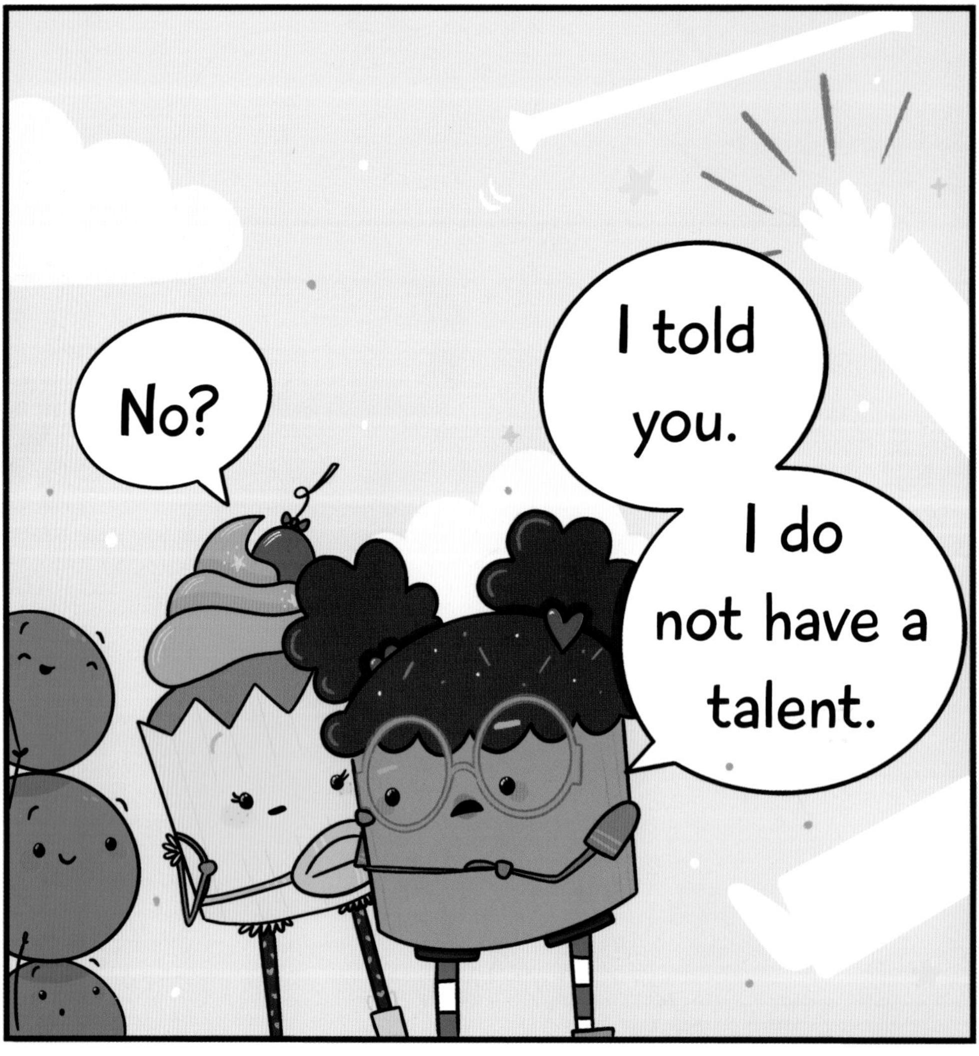
No?
I told you.
I do not have a talent.

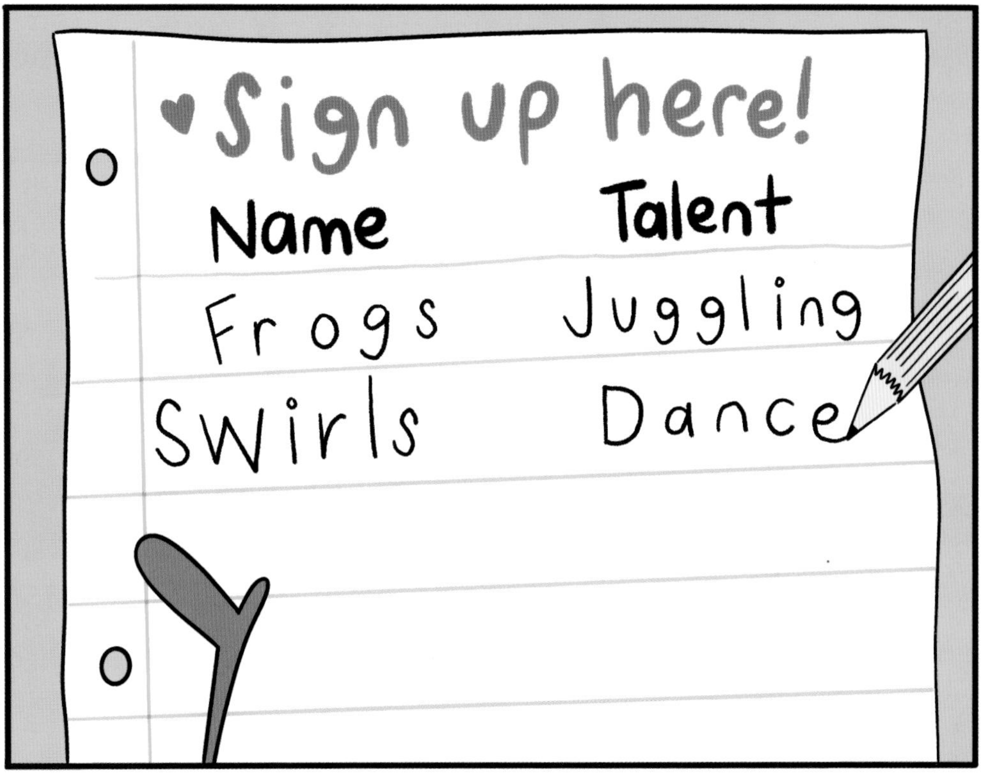
Sign up here!
Name
Talent
Frogs
Juggling
Swirls
Dance

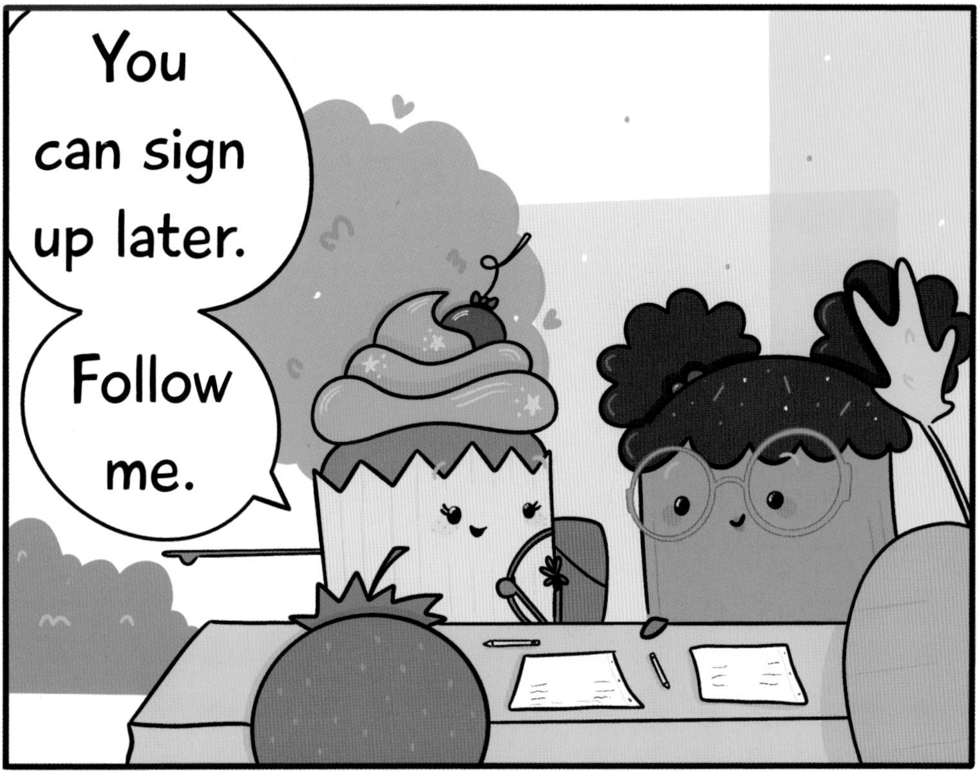
You can sign up later.
Follow me.

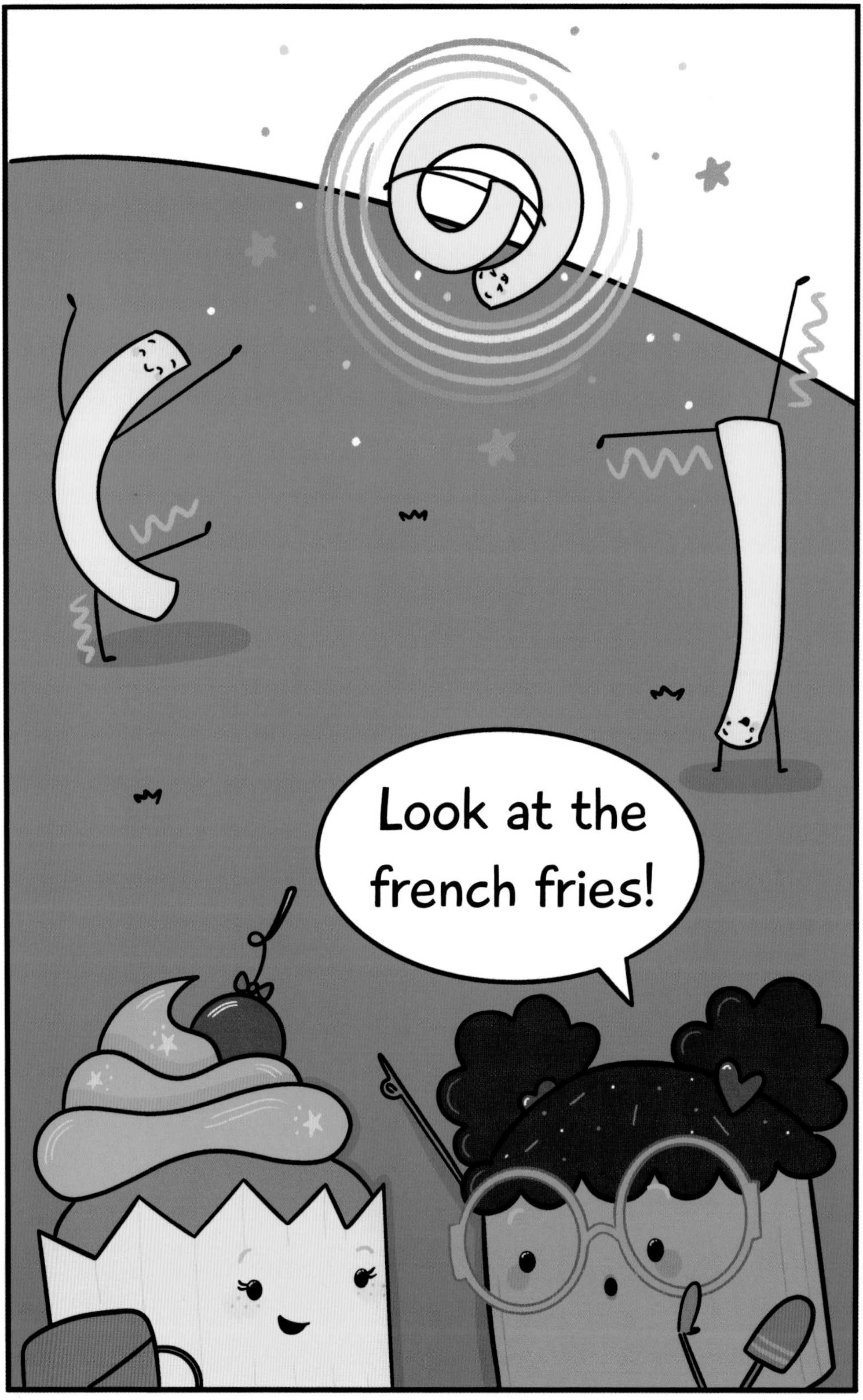
Look at the french fries!

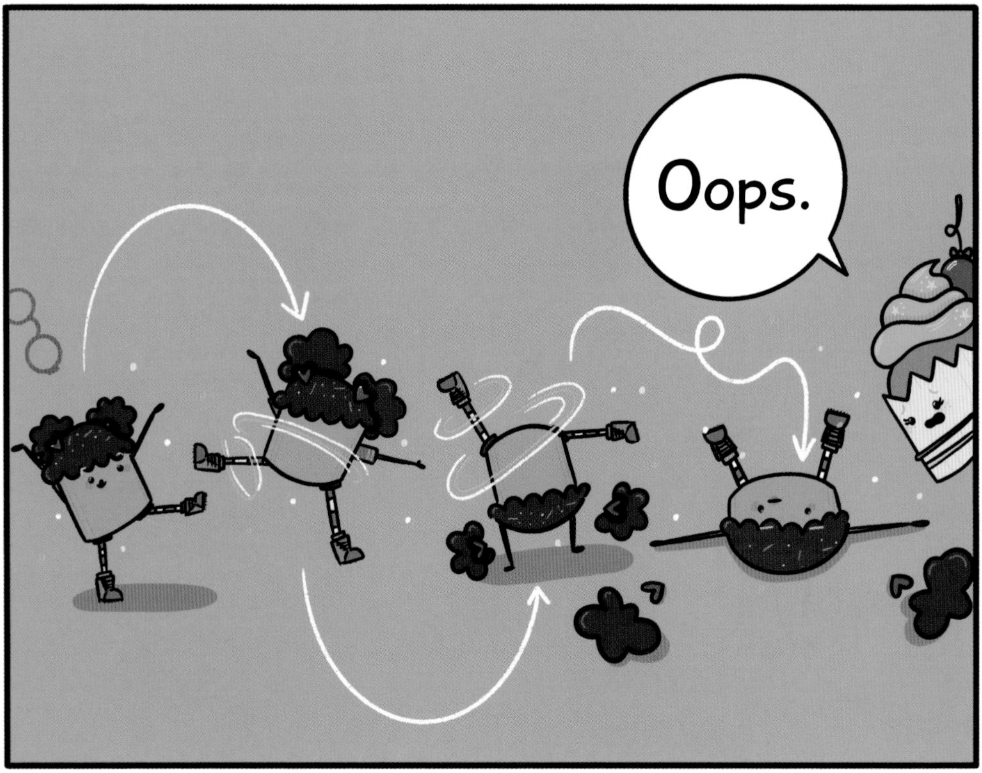
Oops.

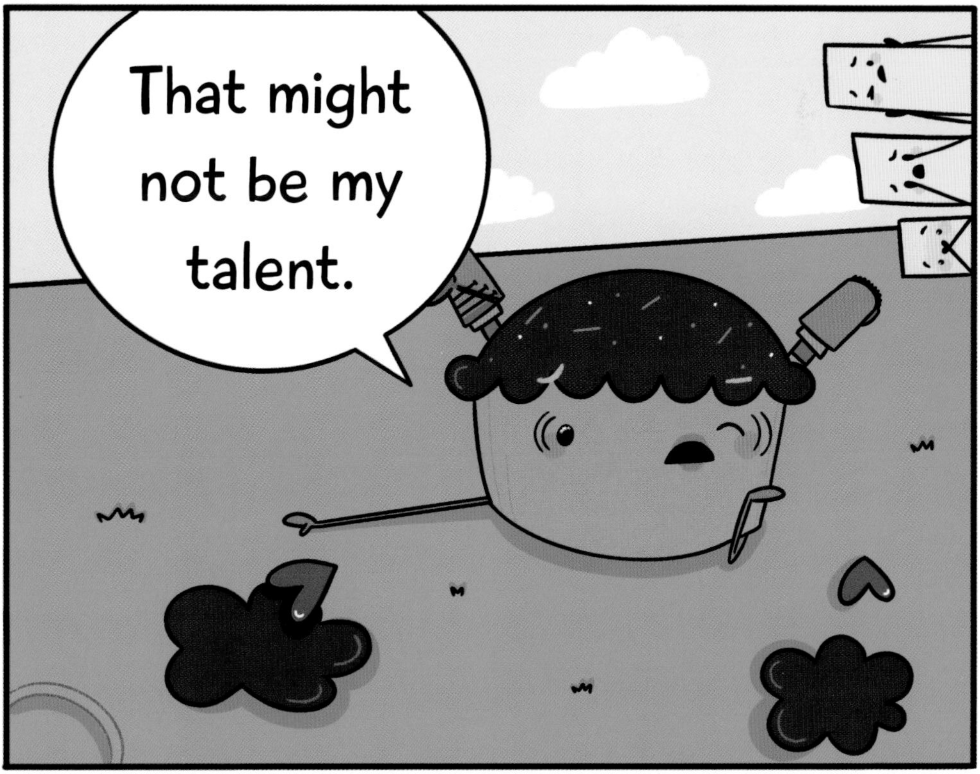
That might not be my talent.

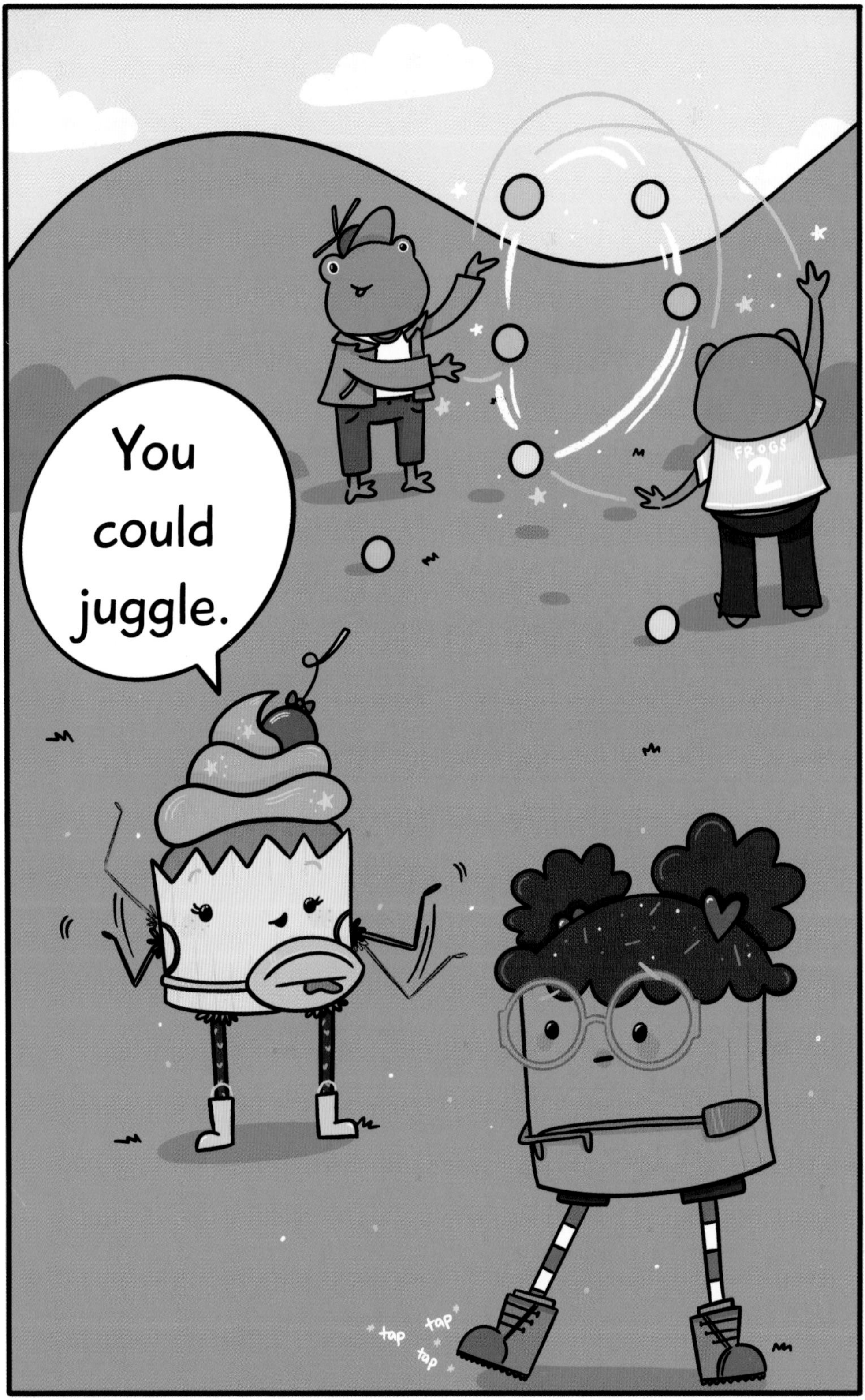
You could juggle.
FROGS 2
tap tap tap

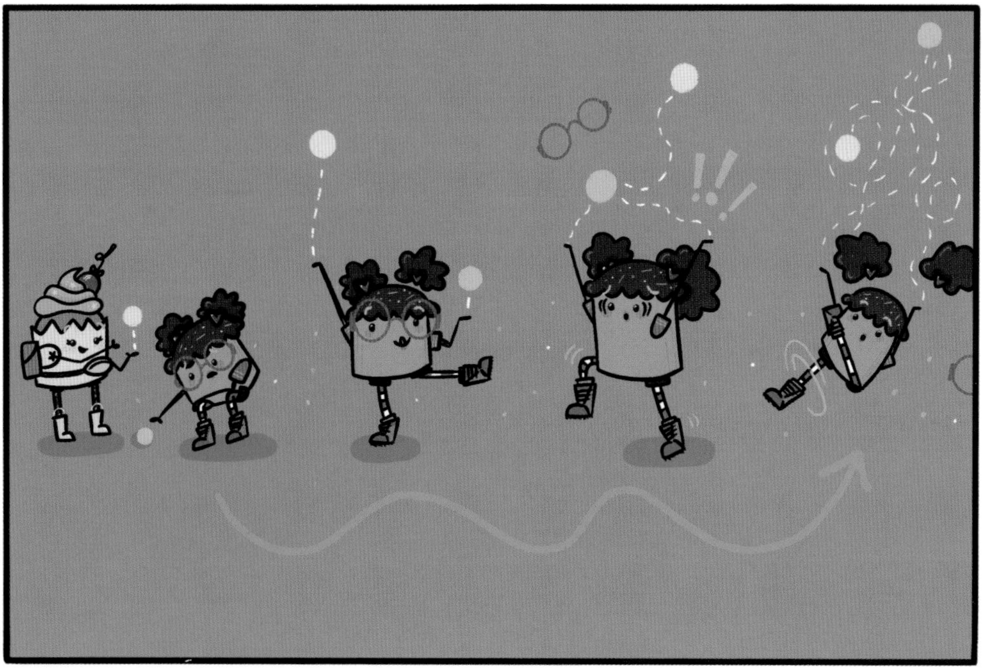

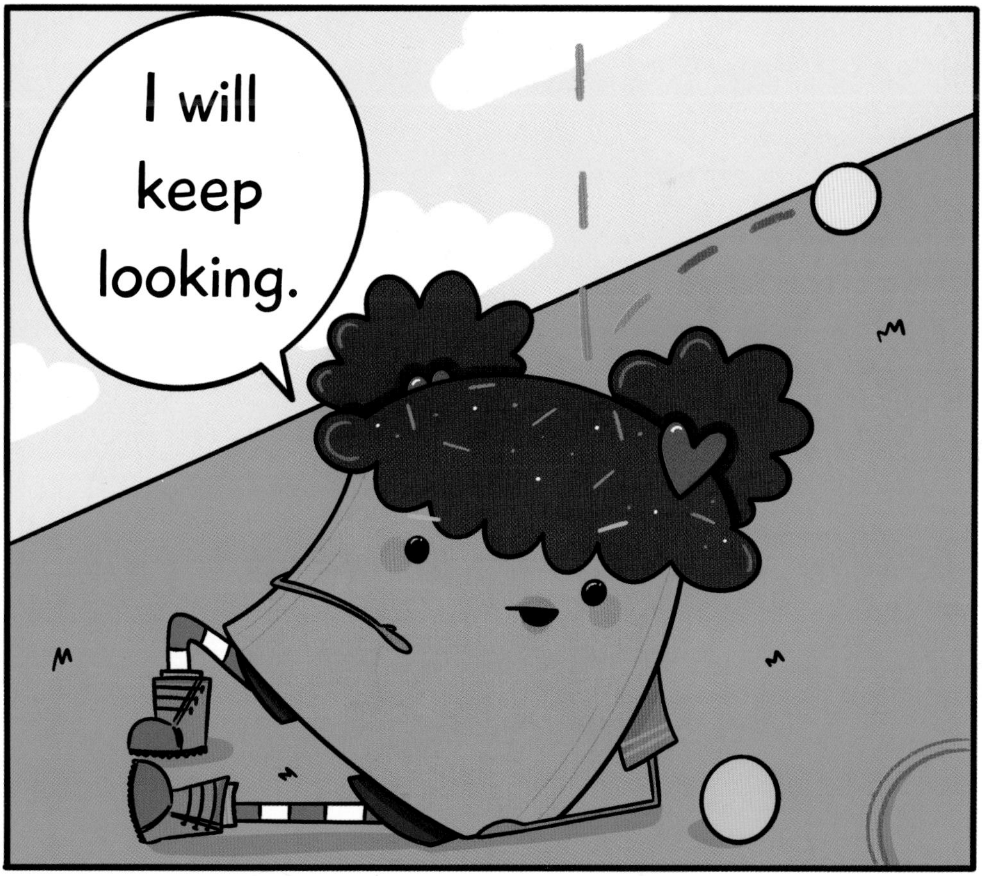
I will keep looking.

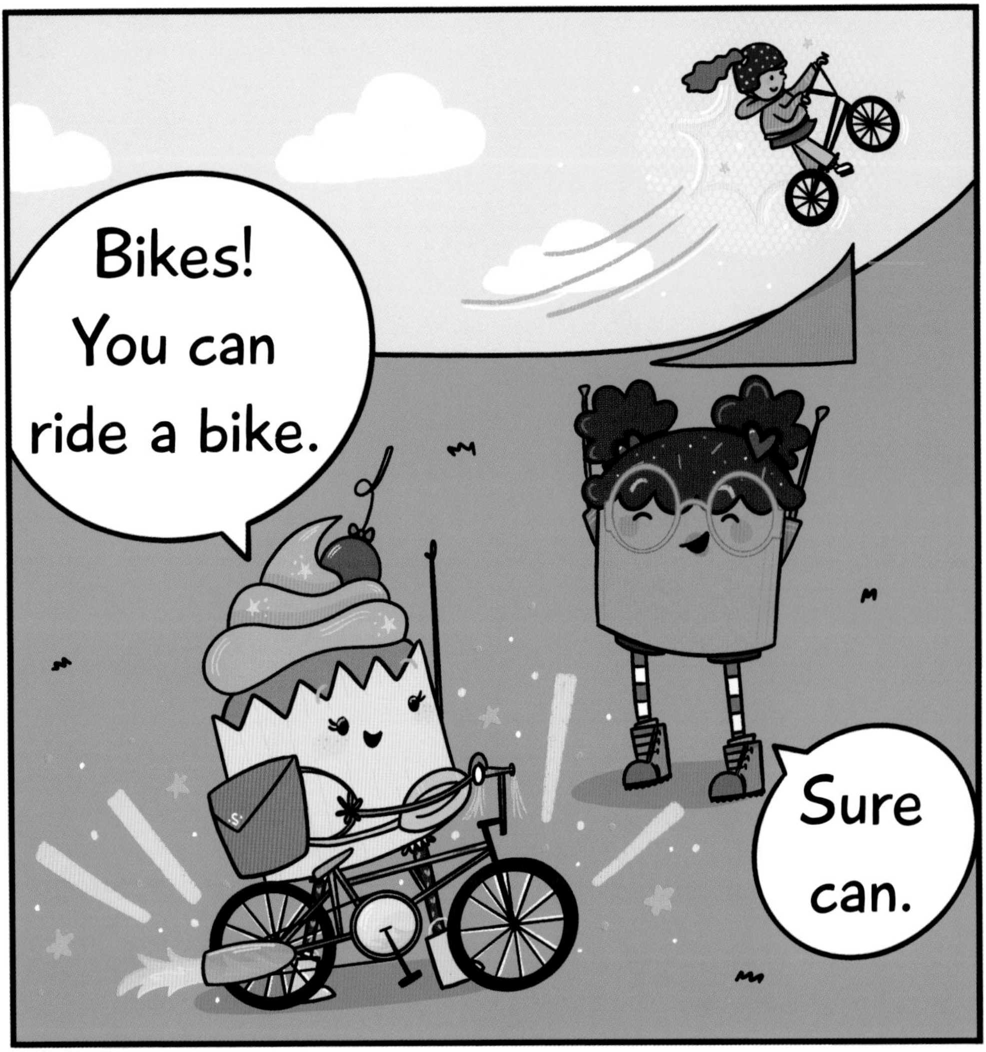
Bikes! You can ride a bike.
Sure can.

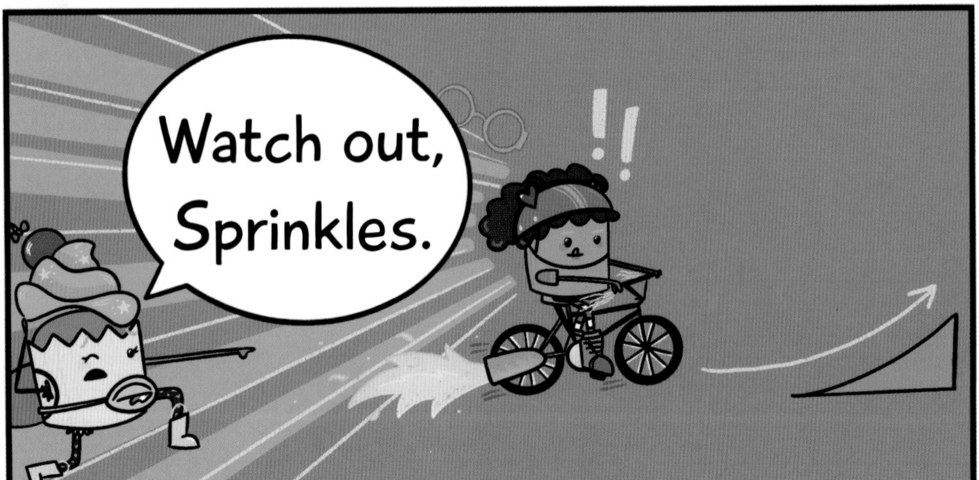
Watch out, Sprinkles.
!!

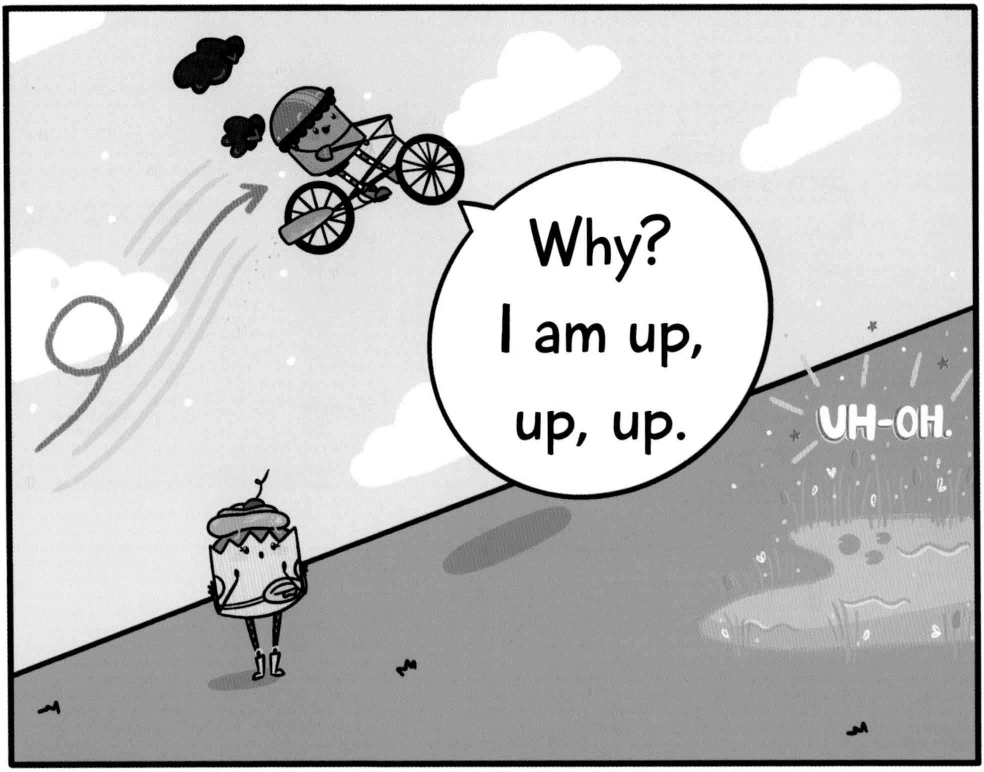
Why? I am up, up, up.
UH-OH.

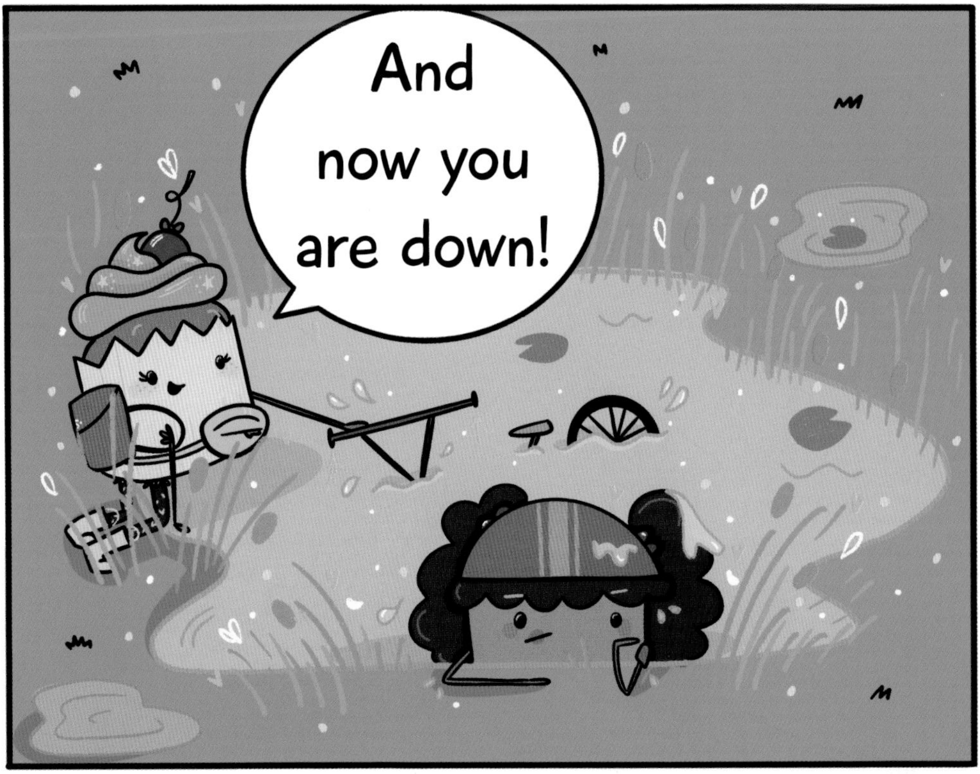
And now you are down!

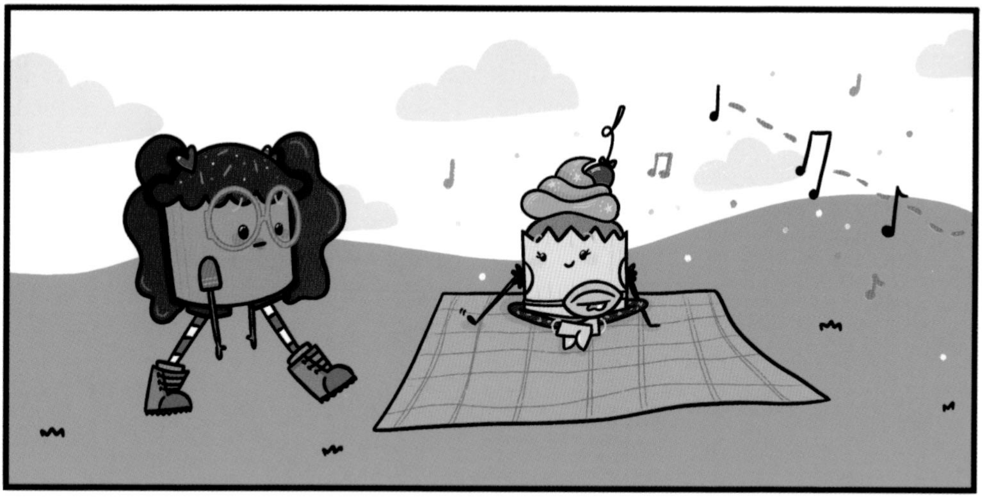

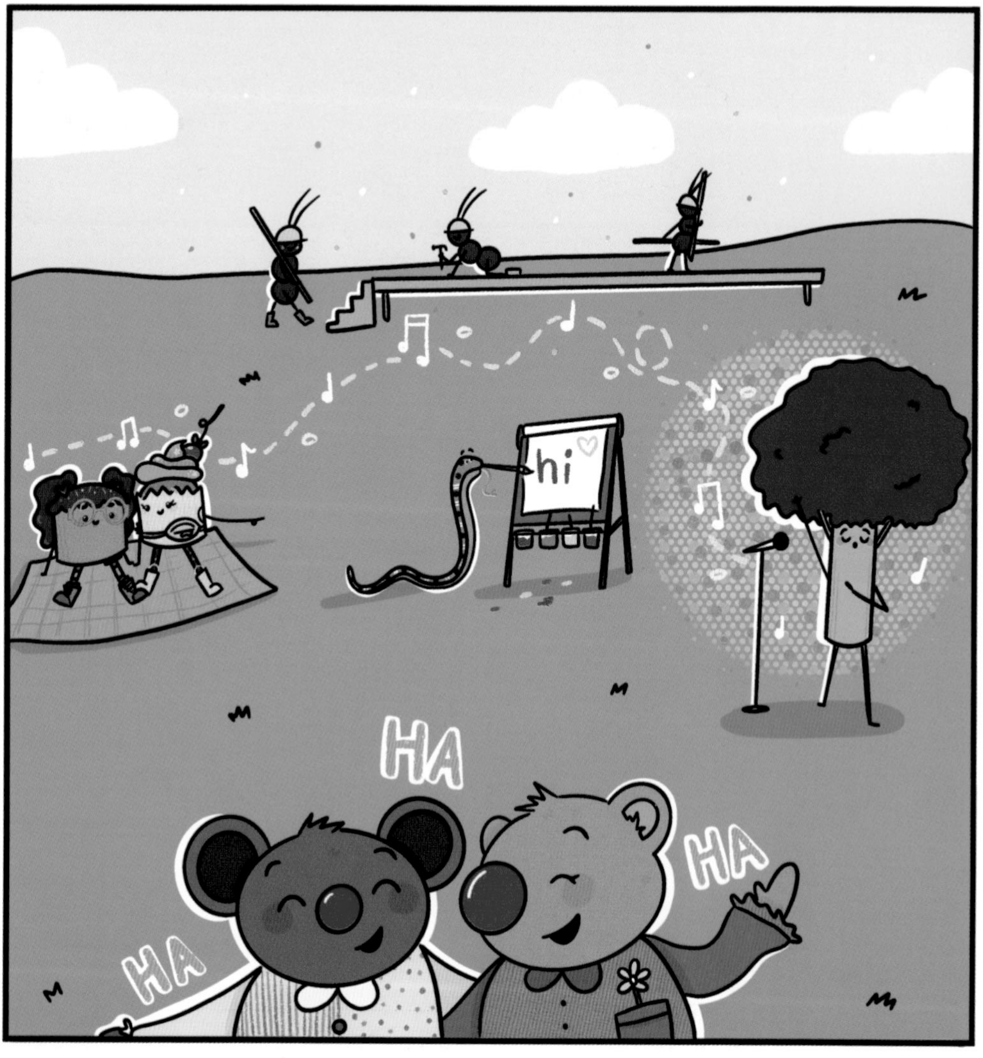
hi
HA
HA
HA

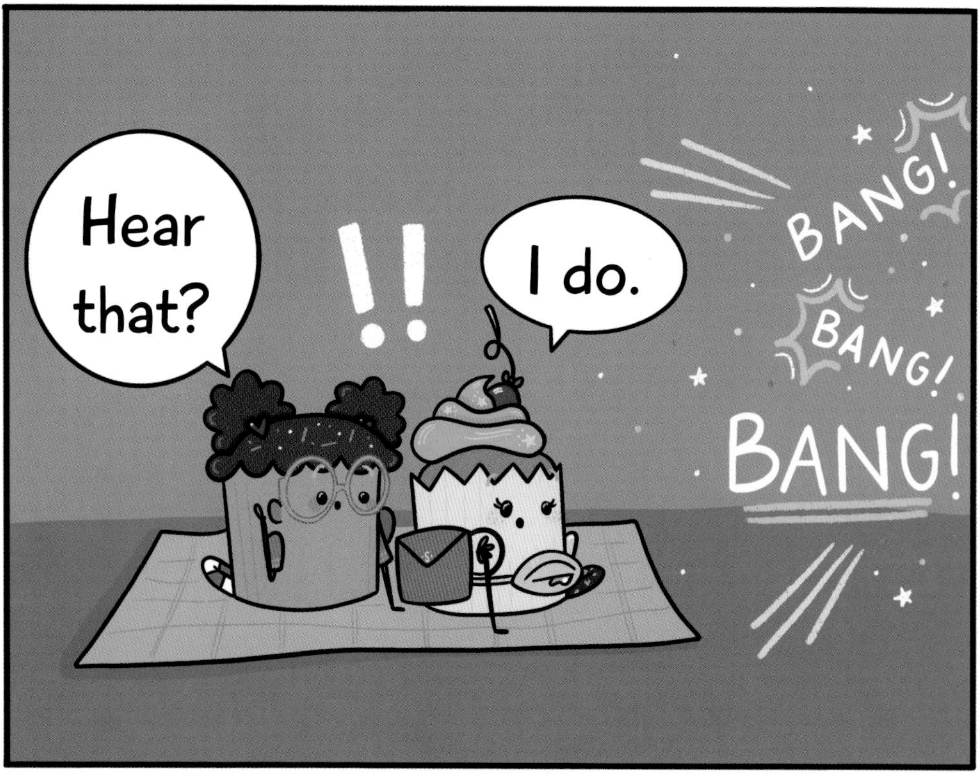
Hear that?
!!
I do.
BANG!
BANG!
BANG!

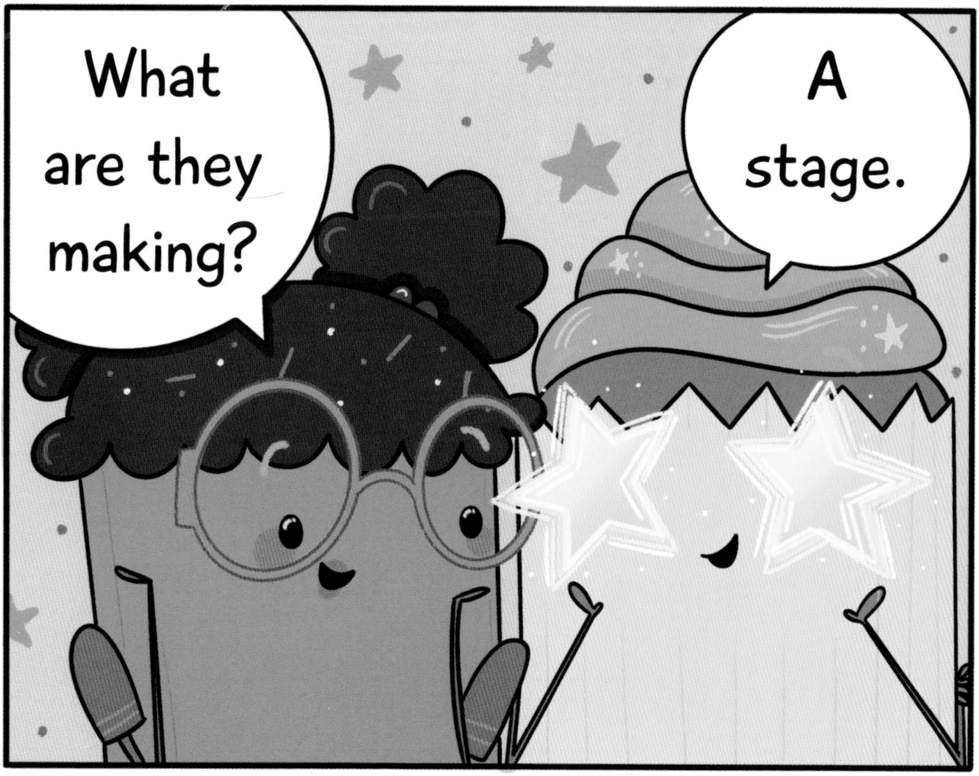
What are they making?
A stage.

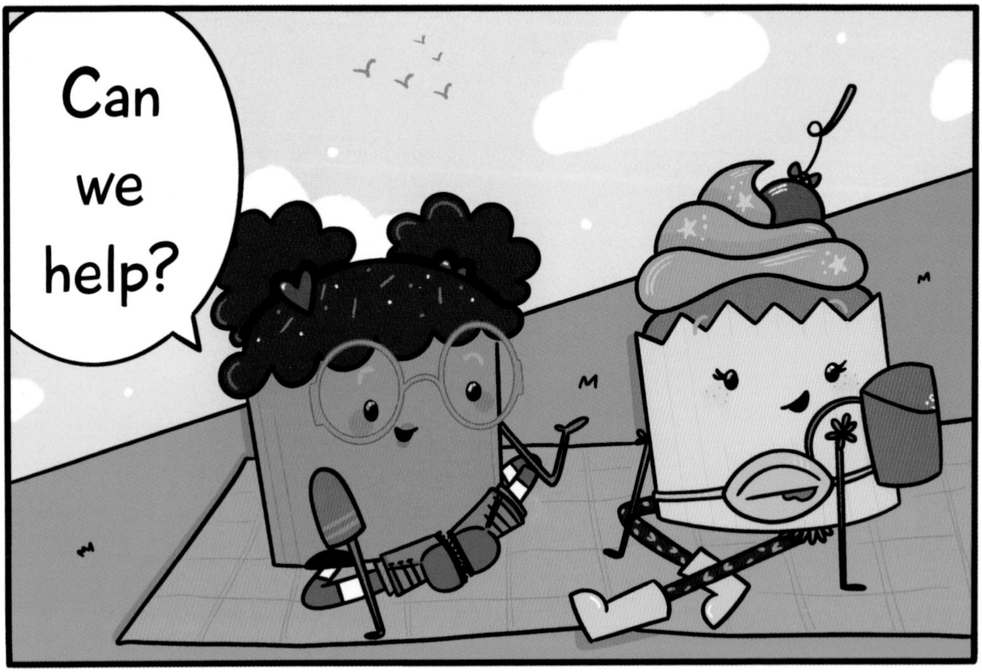
Can we help?

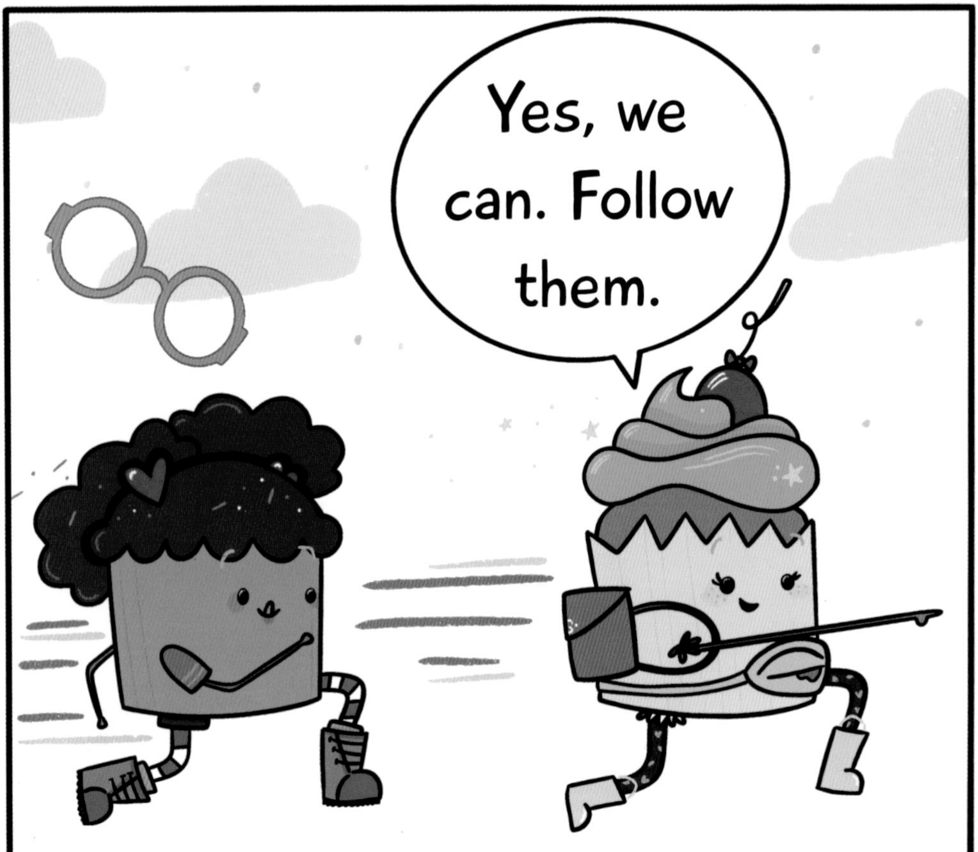
Yes, we can. Follow them.

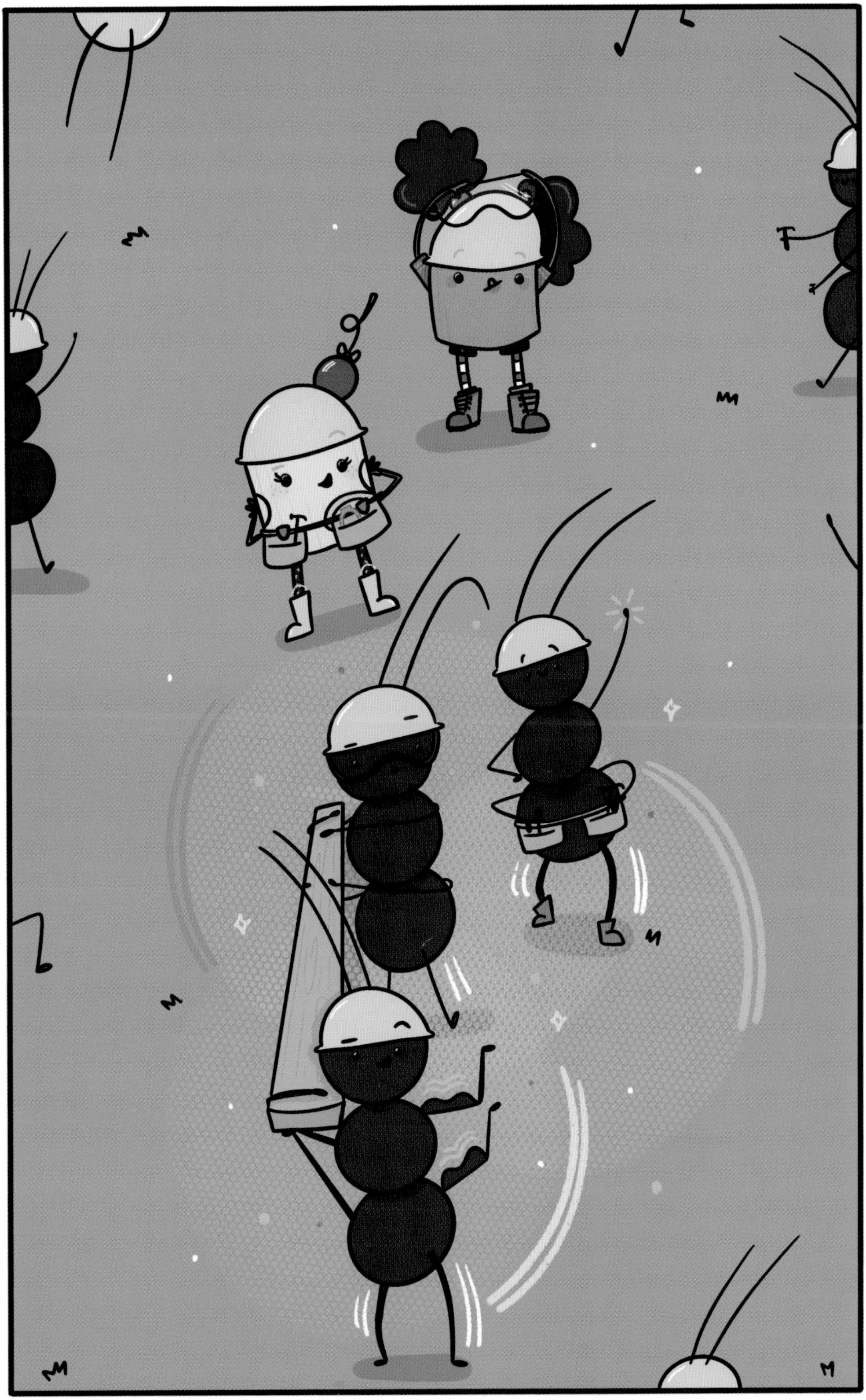

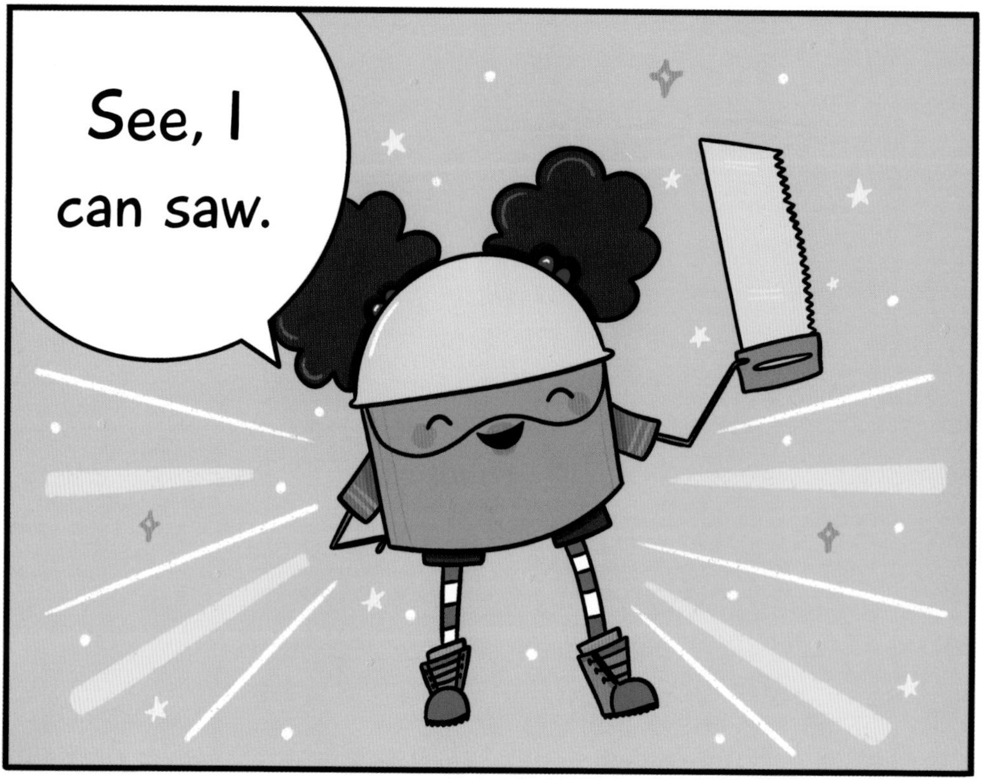
See, I can saw.

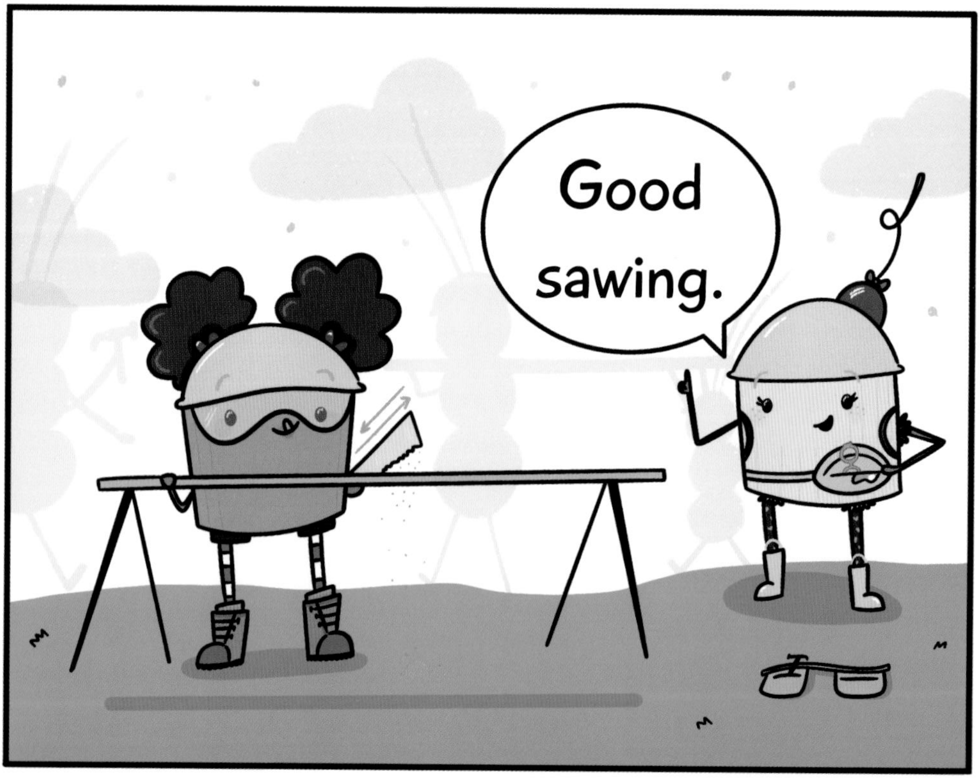
Good sawing.

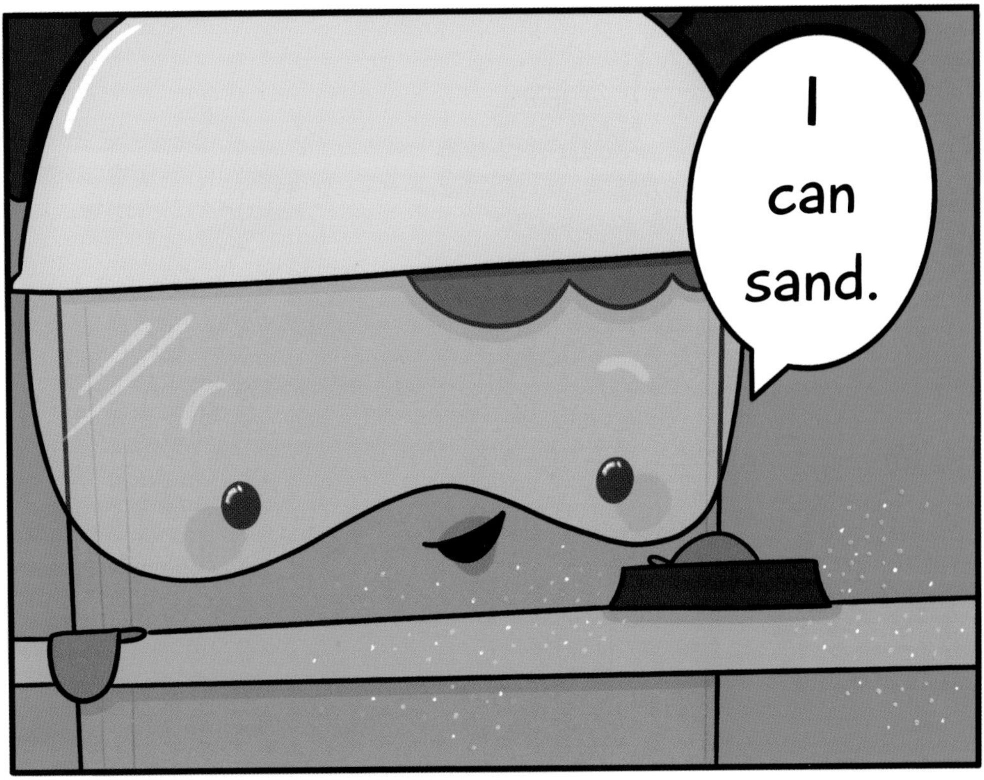
I can sand.

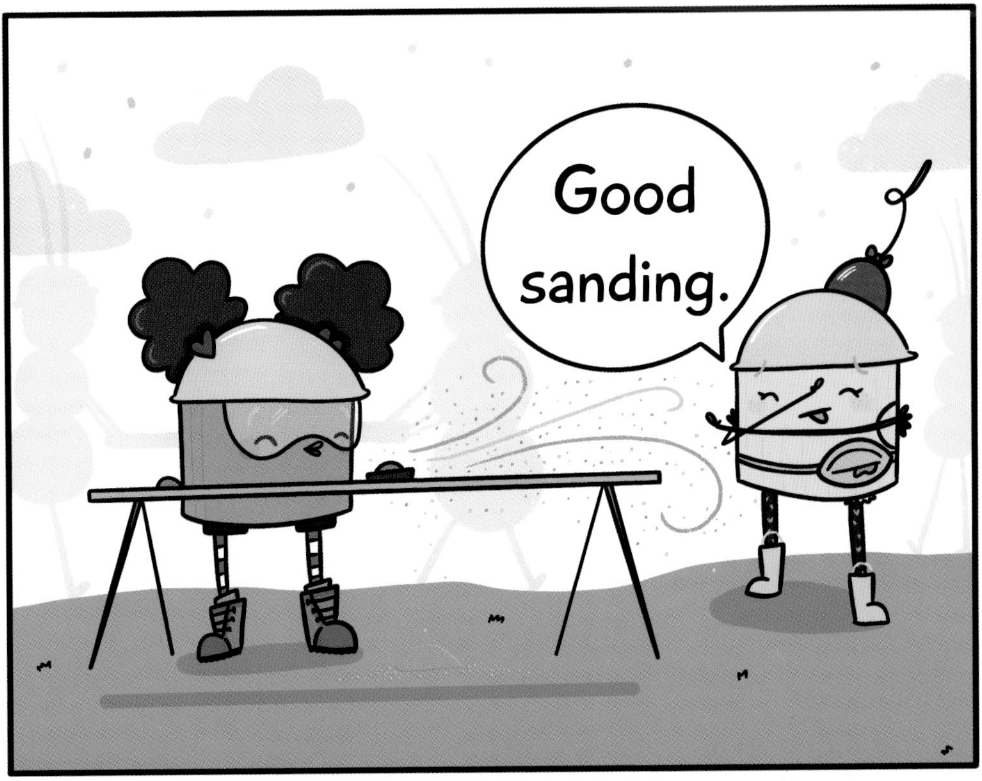
Good sanding.

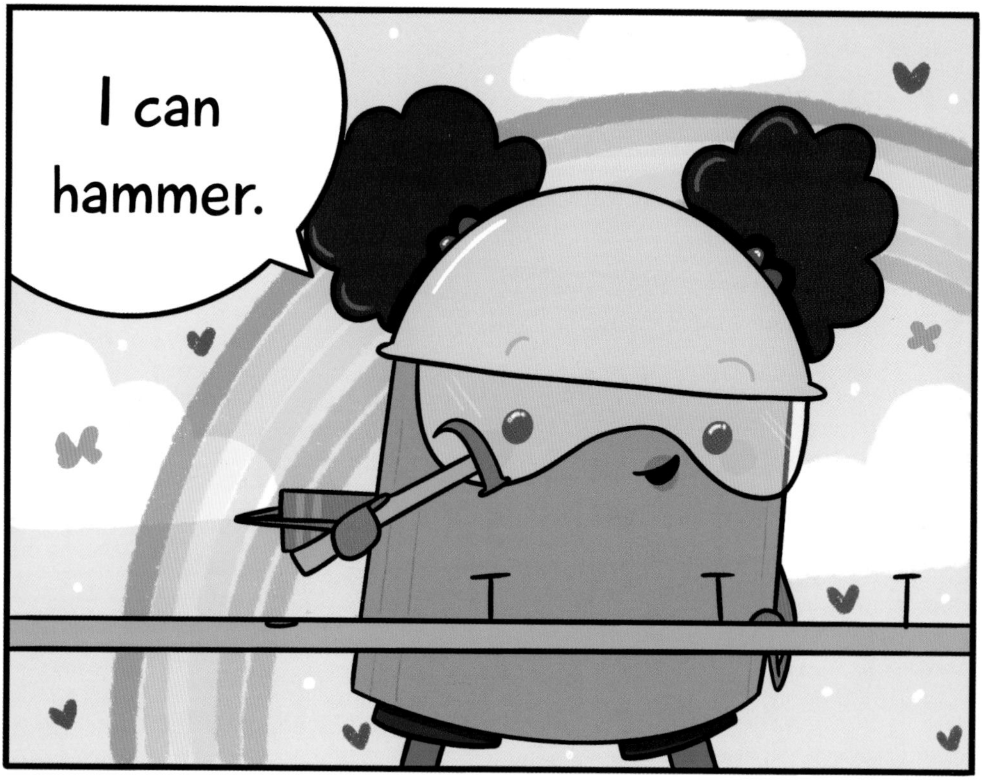
I can hammer.

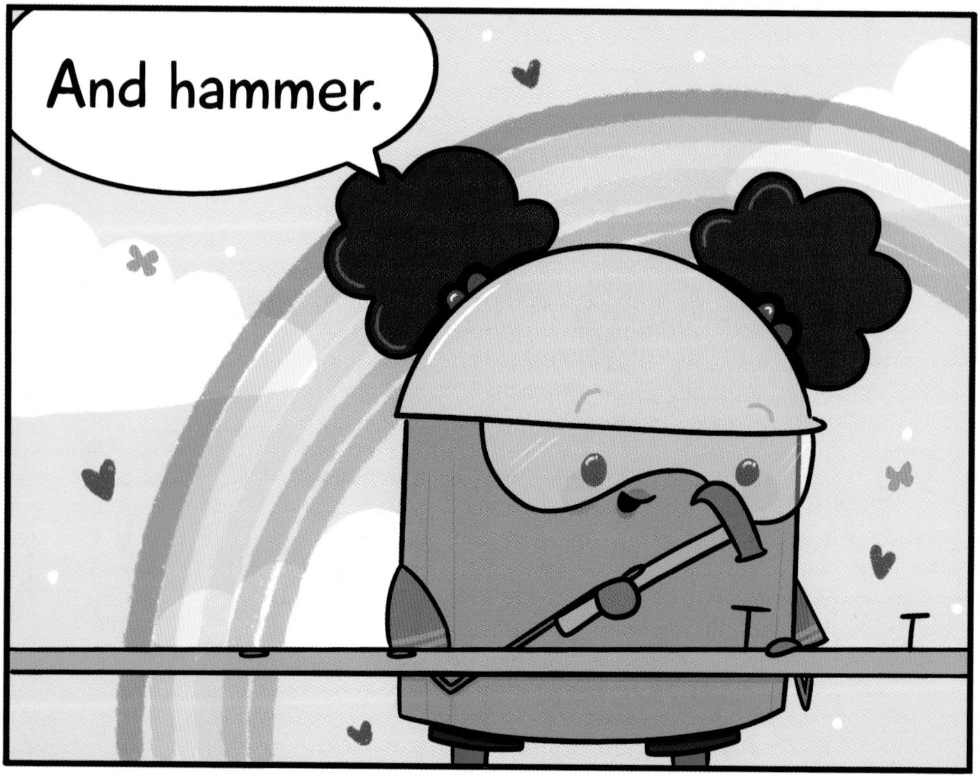
And hammer.

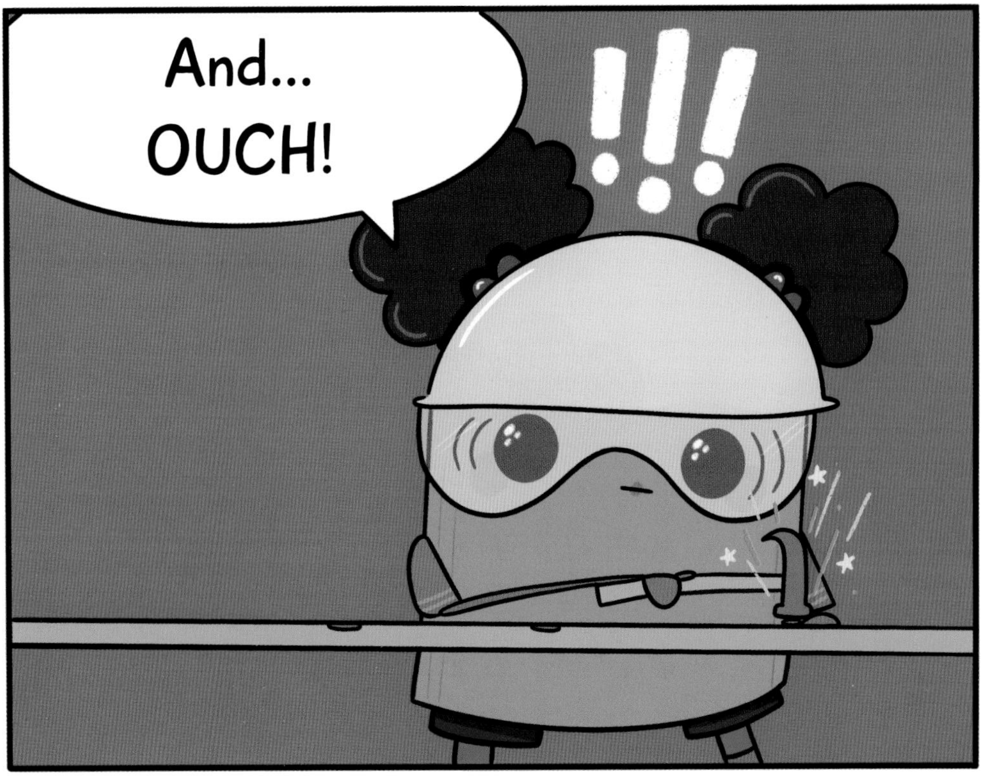
And... OUCH!
!!!

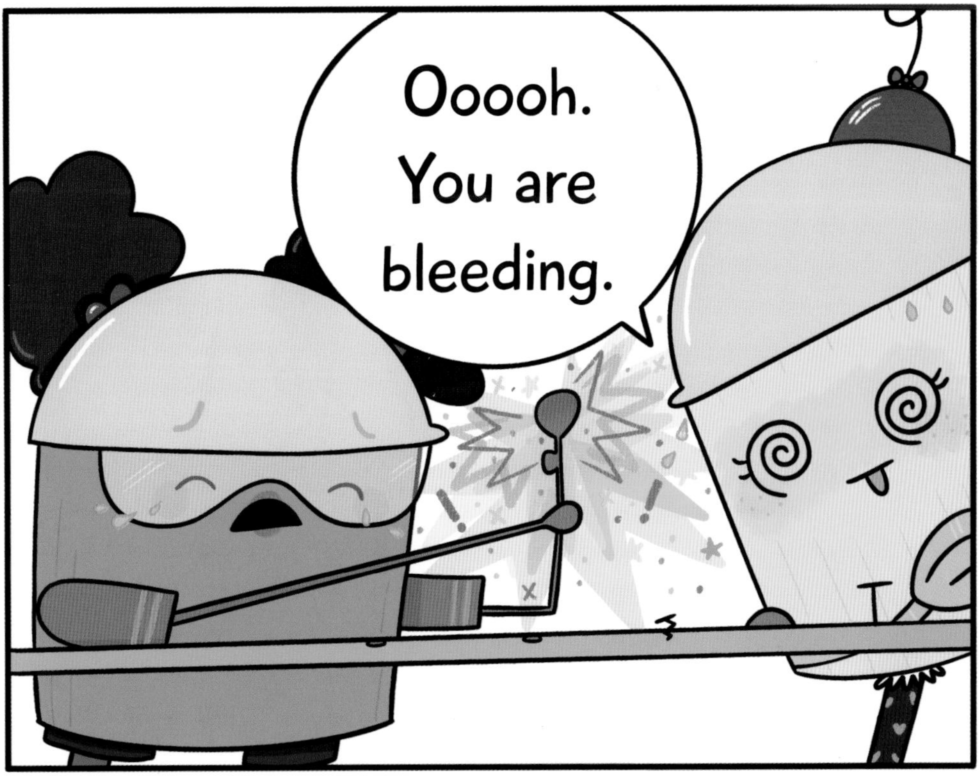
Ooooh. You are bleeding.

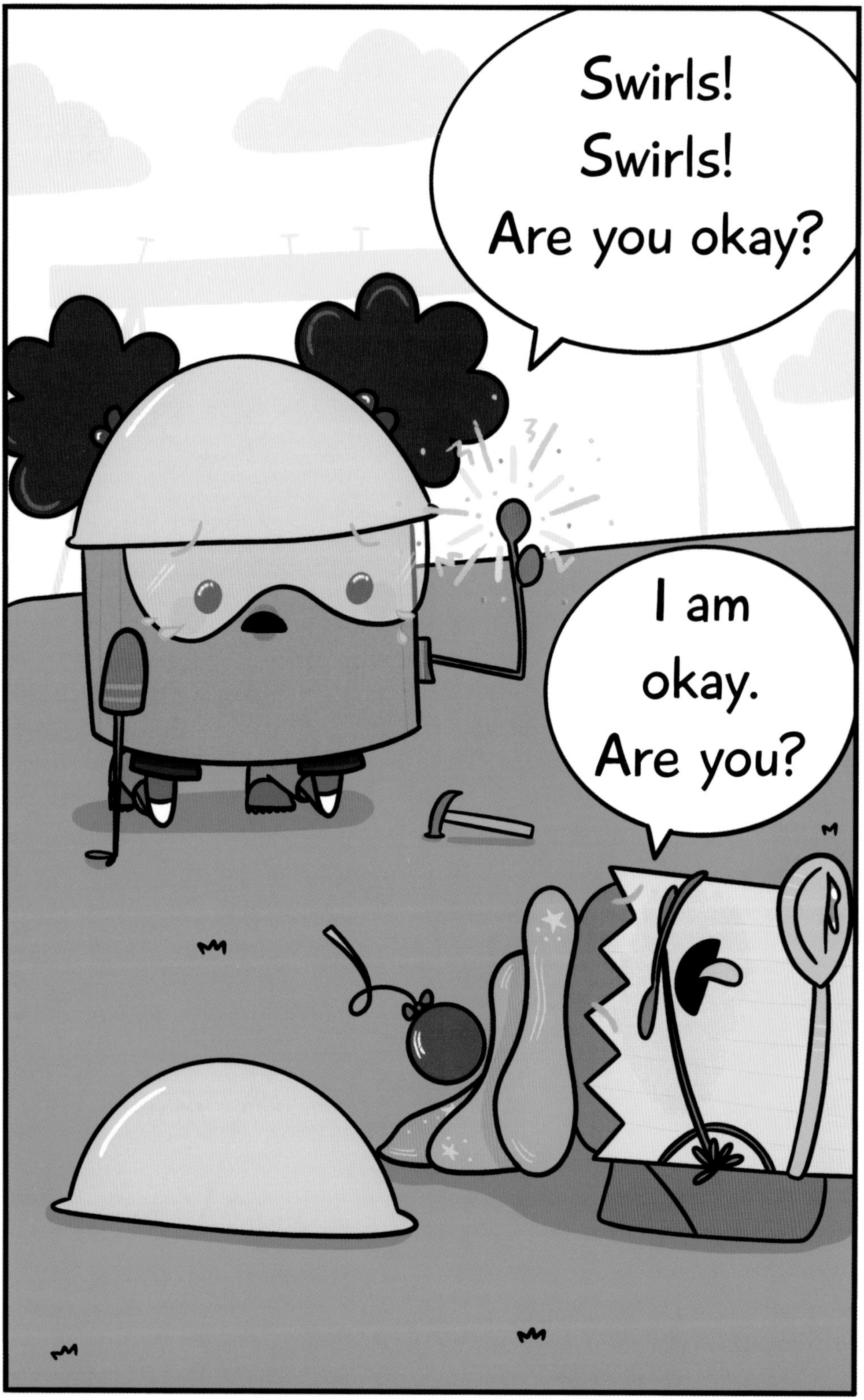
Swirls! Swirls! Are you okay?
I am okay. Are you?

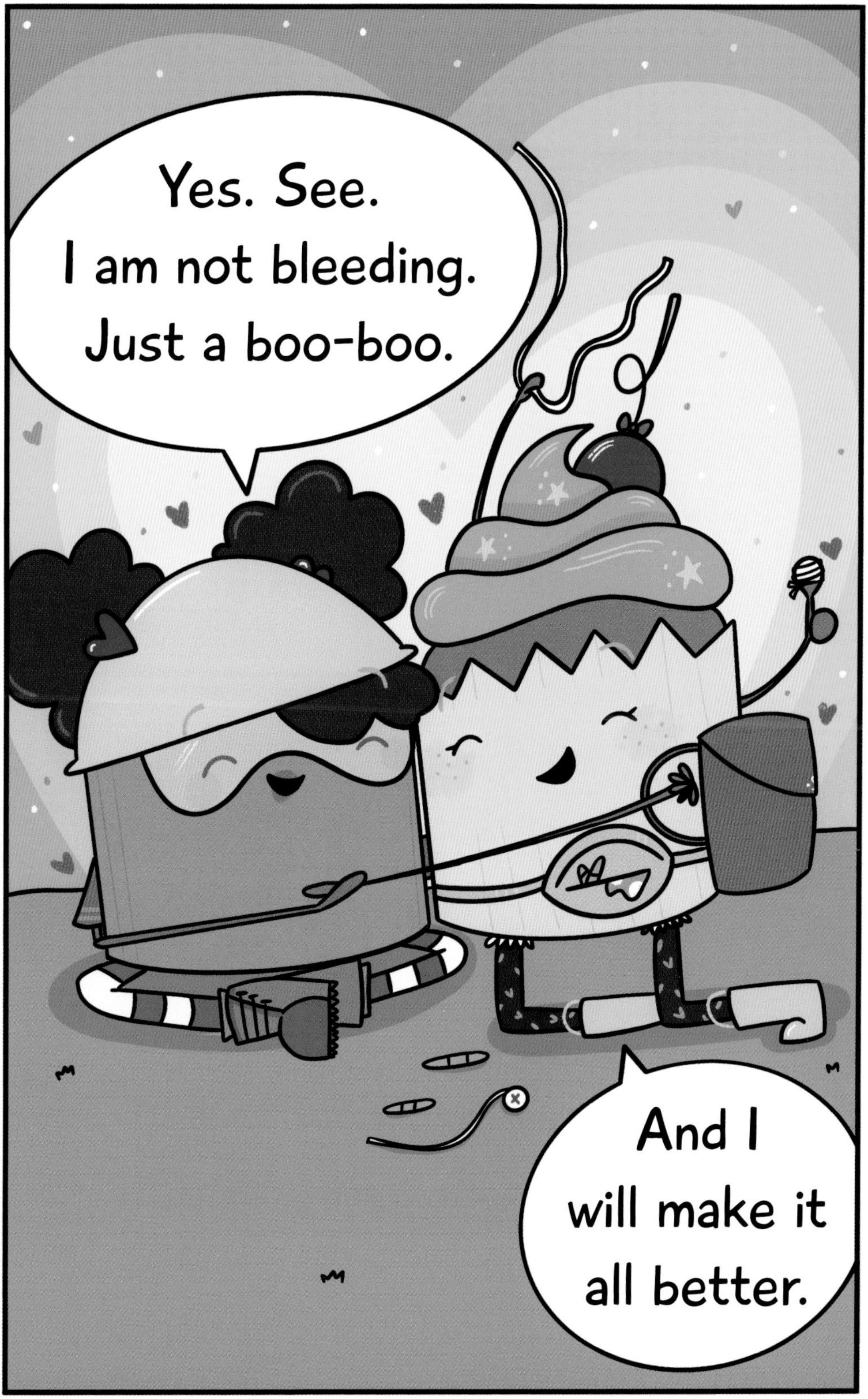
Yes. See.
I am not bleeding.
Just a boo-boo.
And I
will make it
all better.

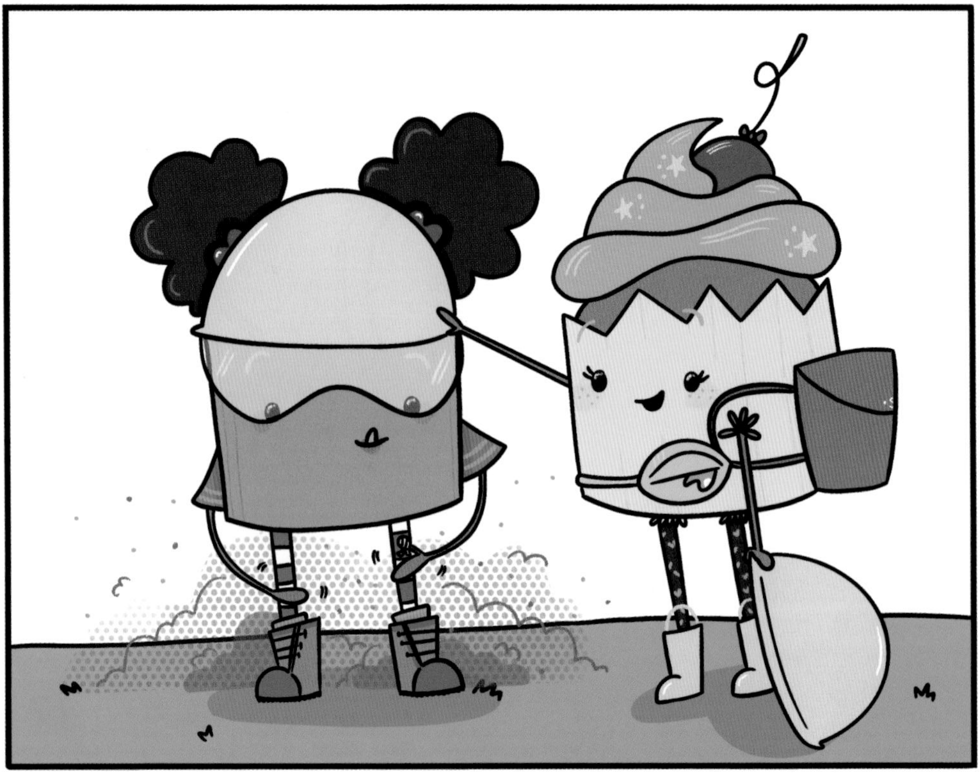

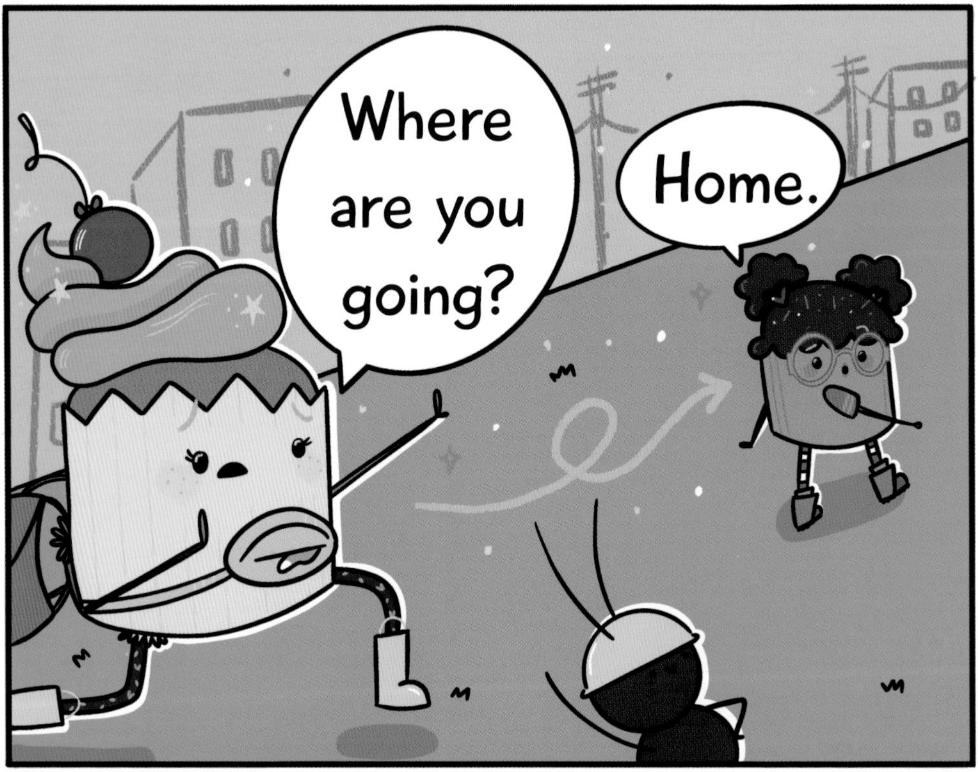
Where are you going?
Home.

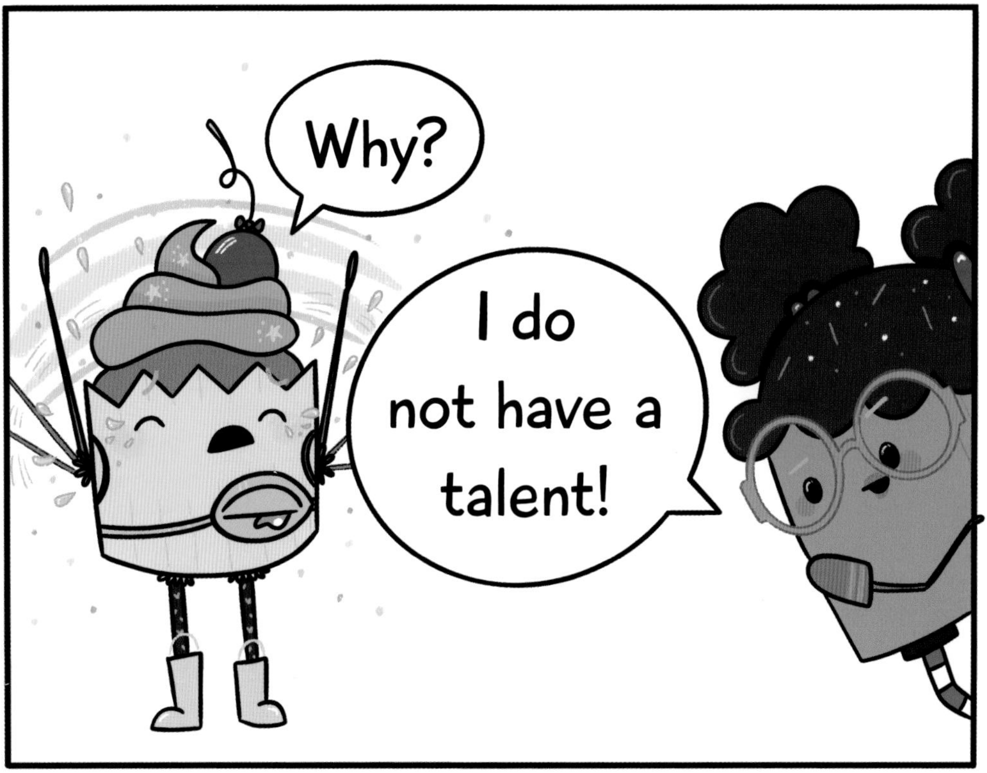
Why?
I do not have a talent!

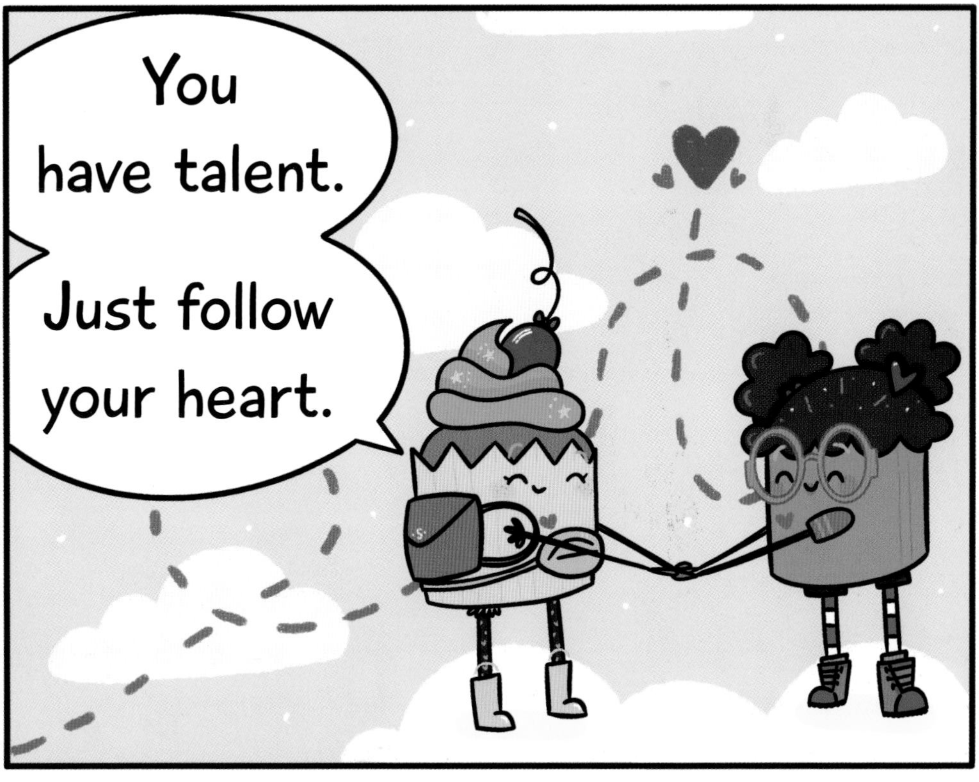
You have talent.
Just follow your heart.

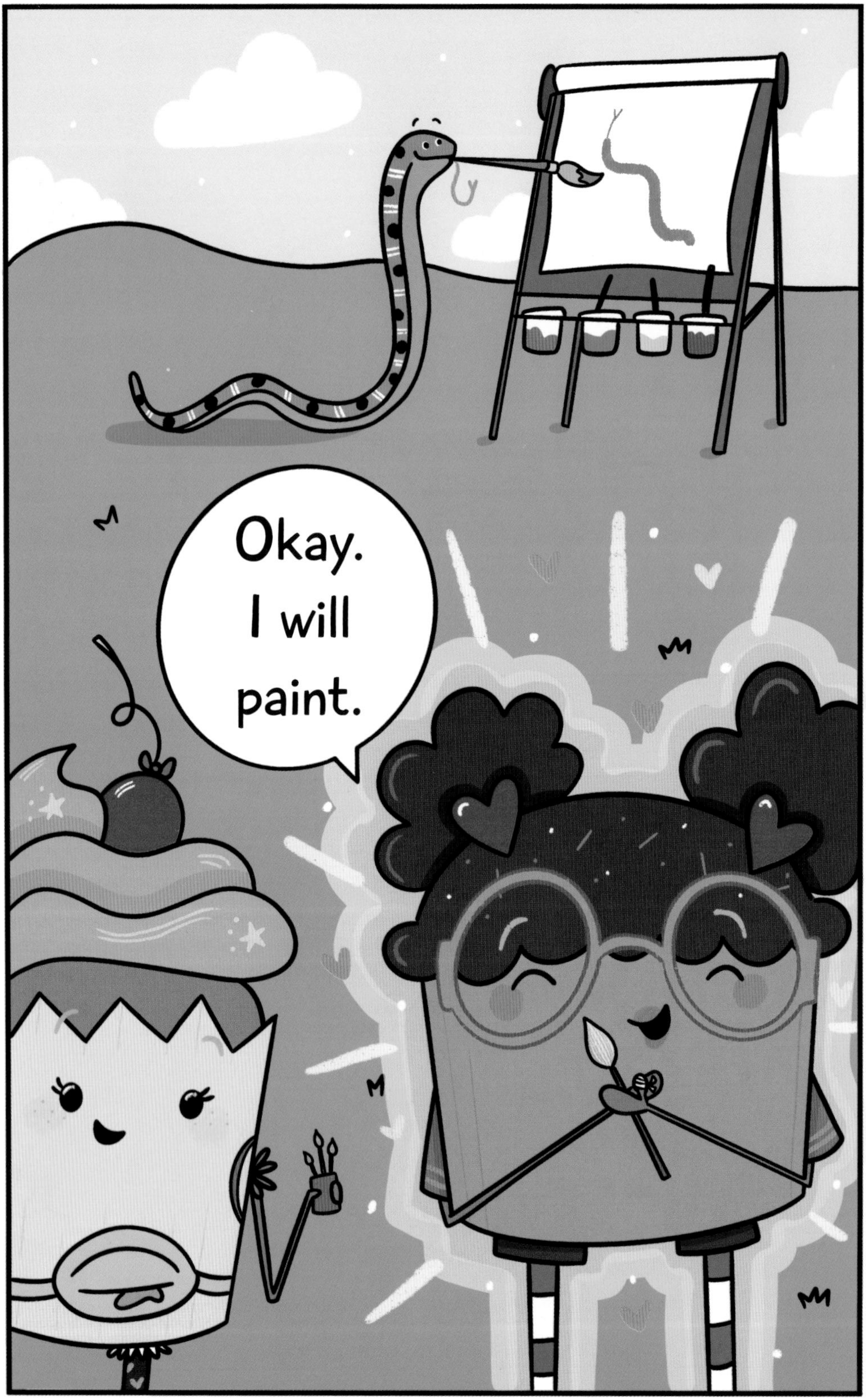
Okay. I will paint.

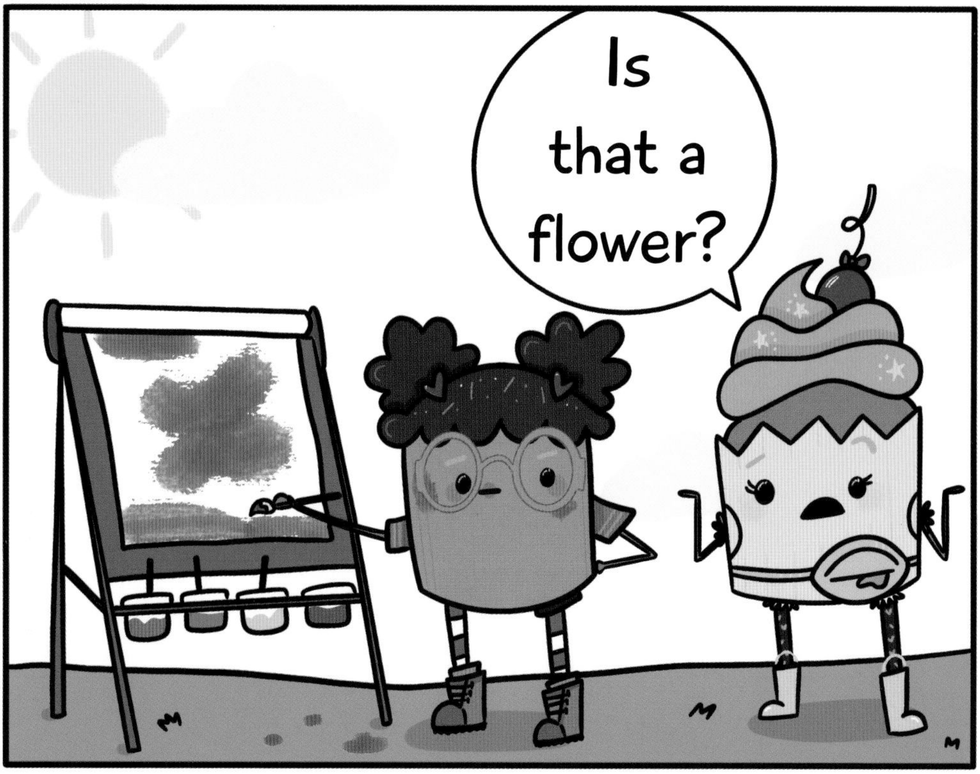
Is that a flower?

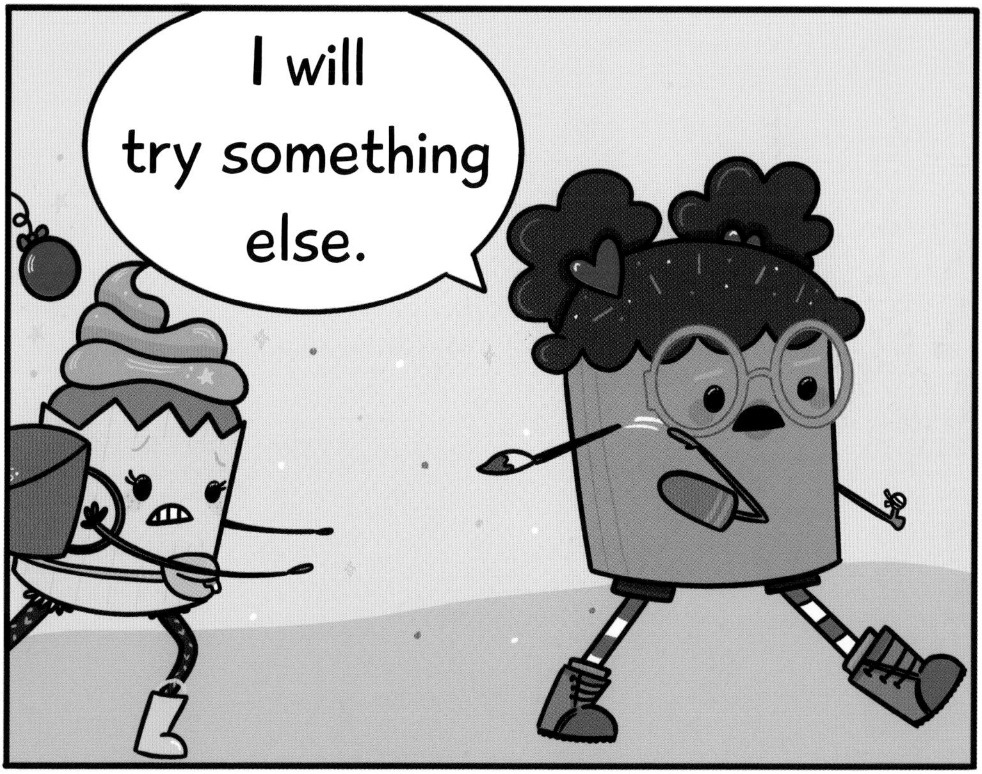
I will try something else.

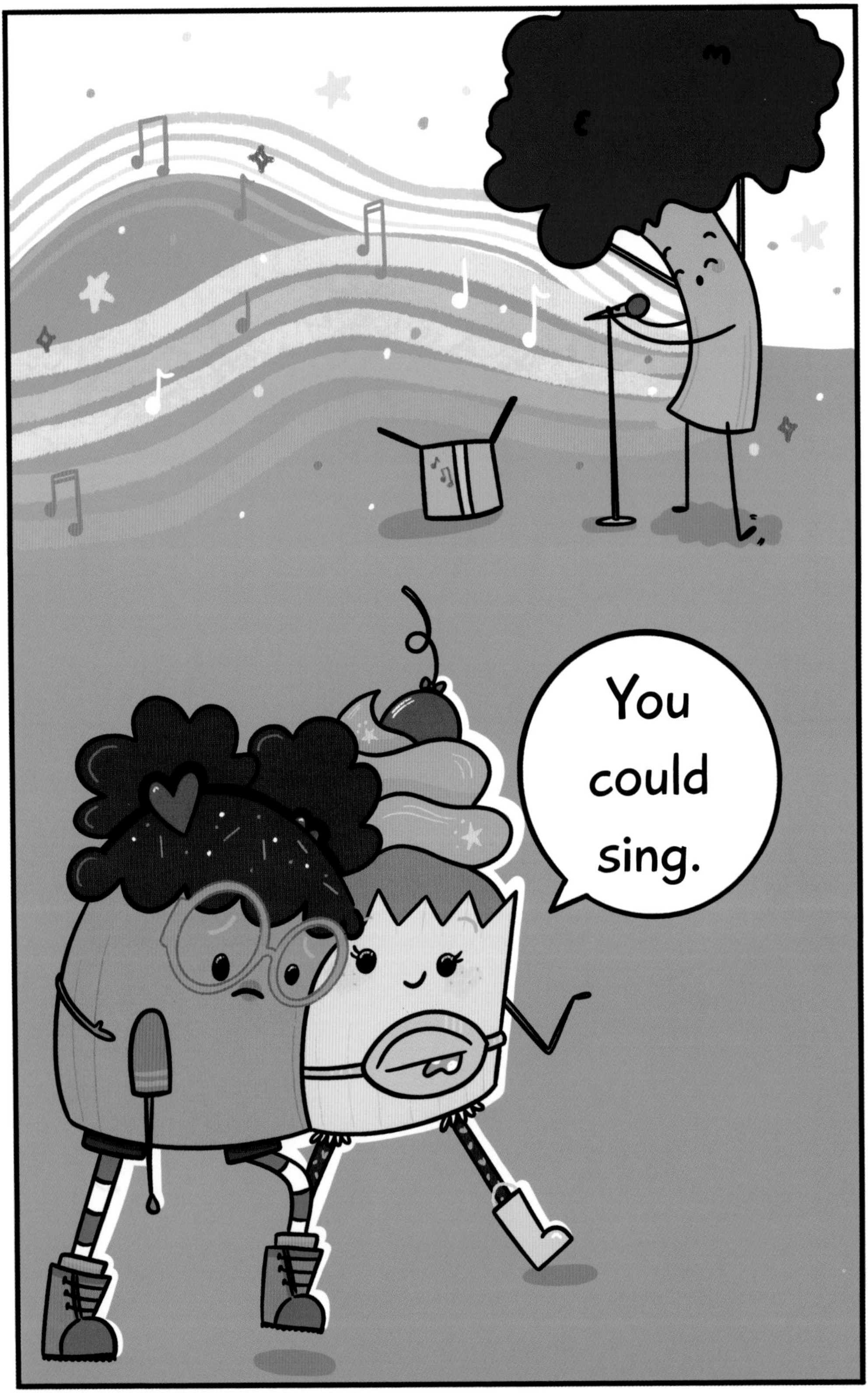
You could sing.

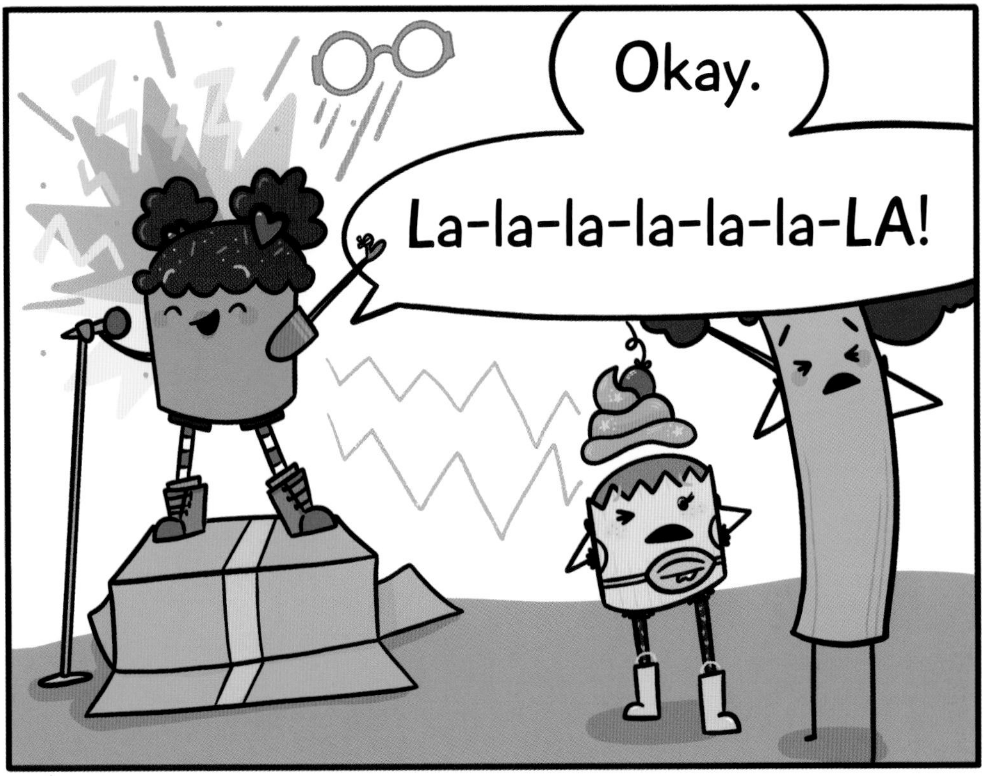
Okay.
La-la-la-la-la-la-LA!
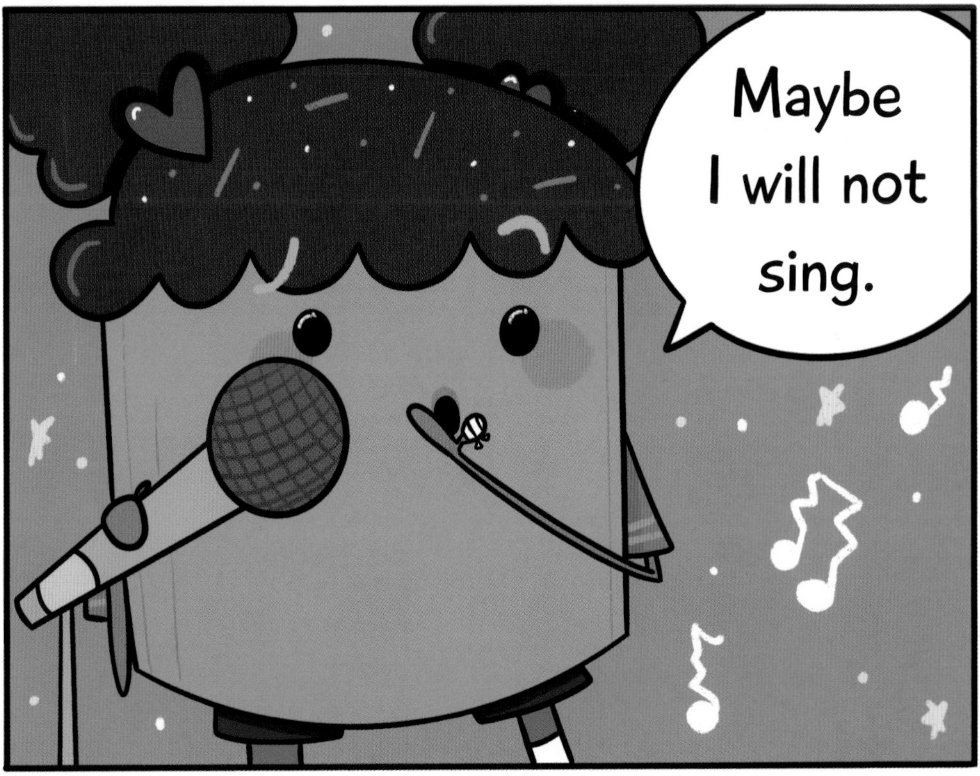
Maybe I will not sing.

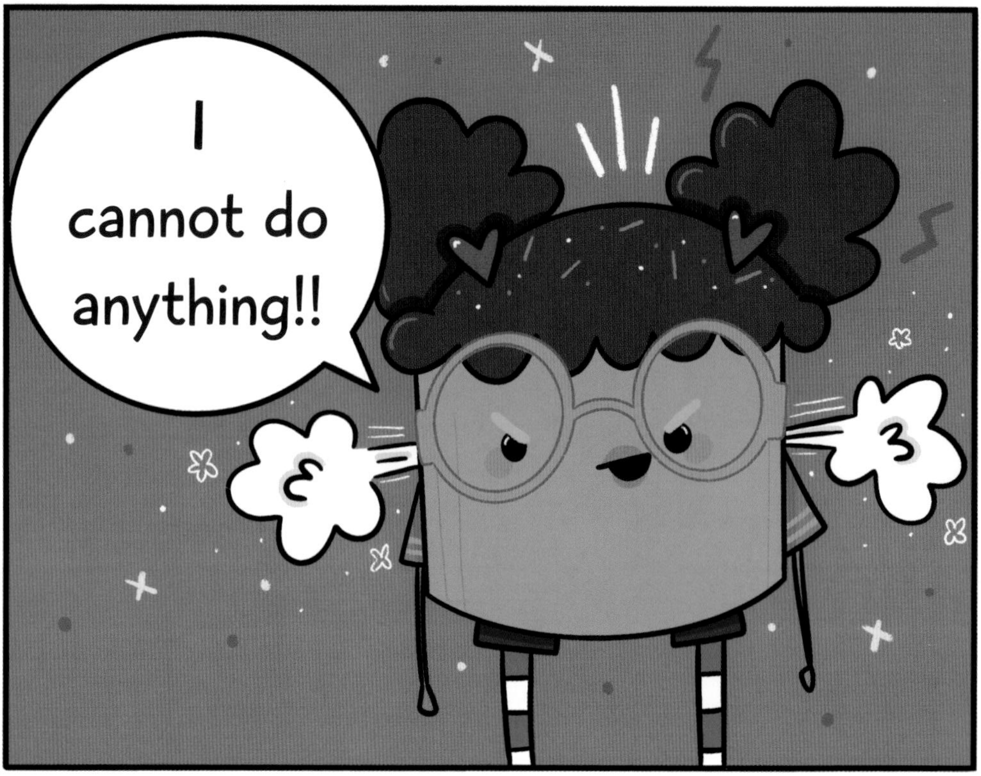
I cannot do anything!!

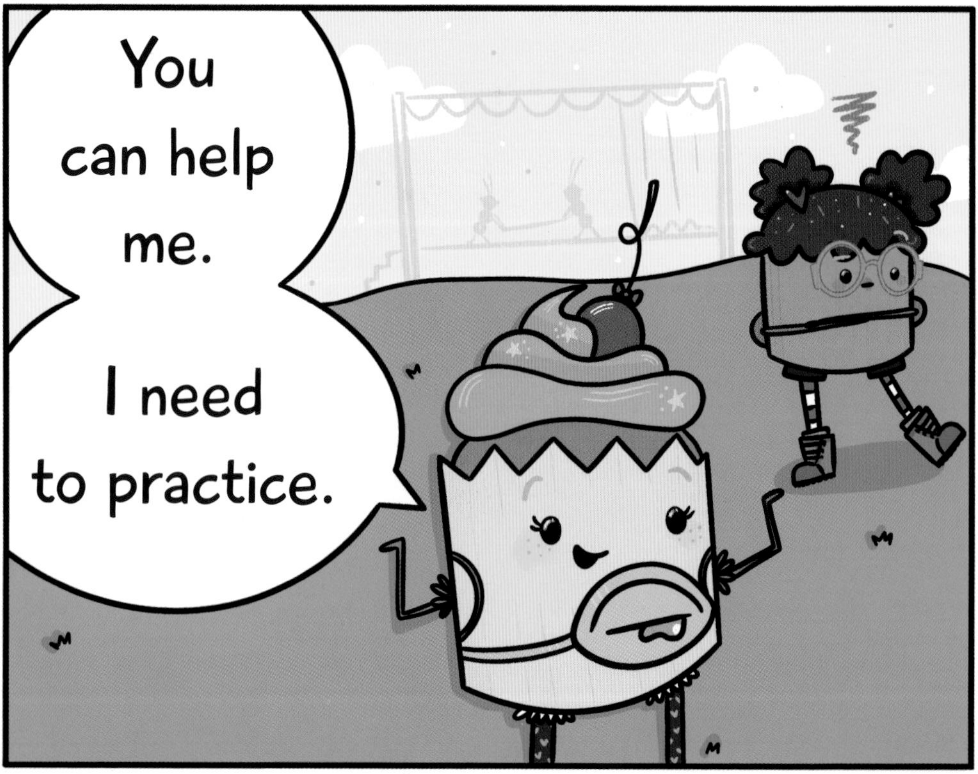
You can help me.
I need to practice.

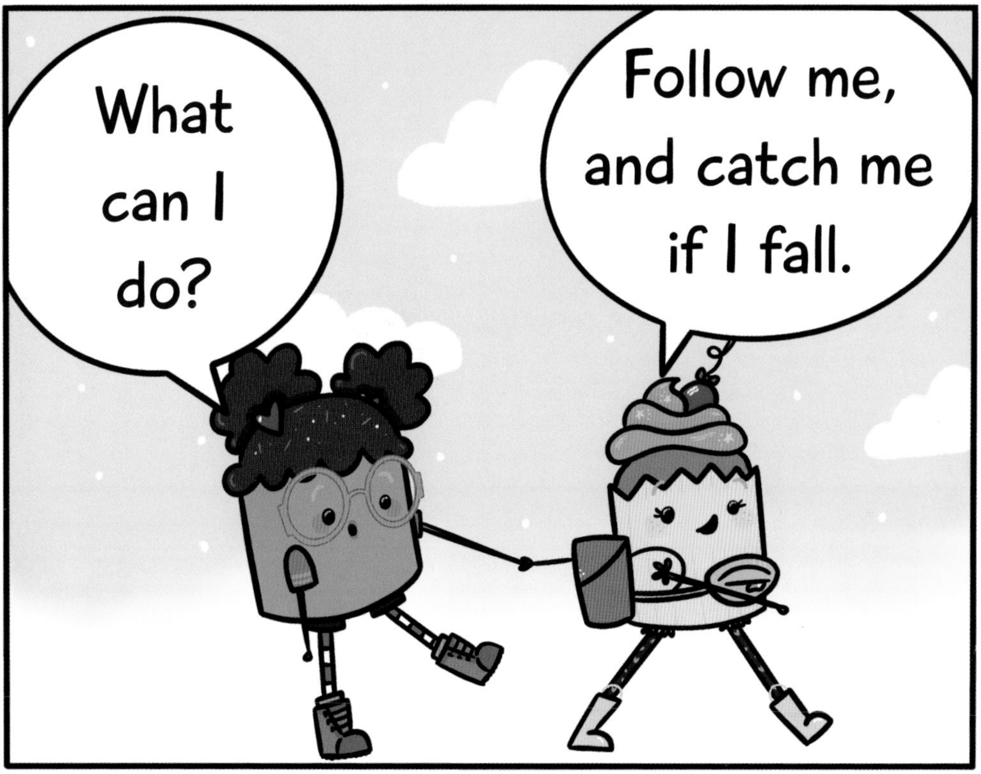
What can I do?
Follow me, and catch me if I fall.

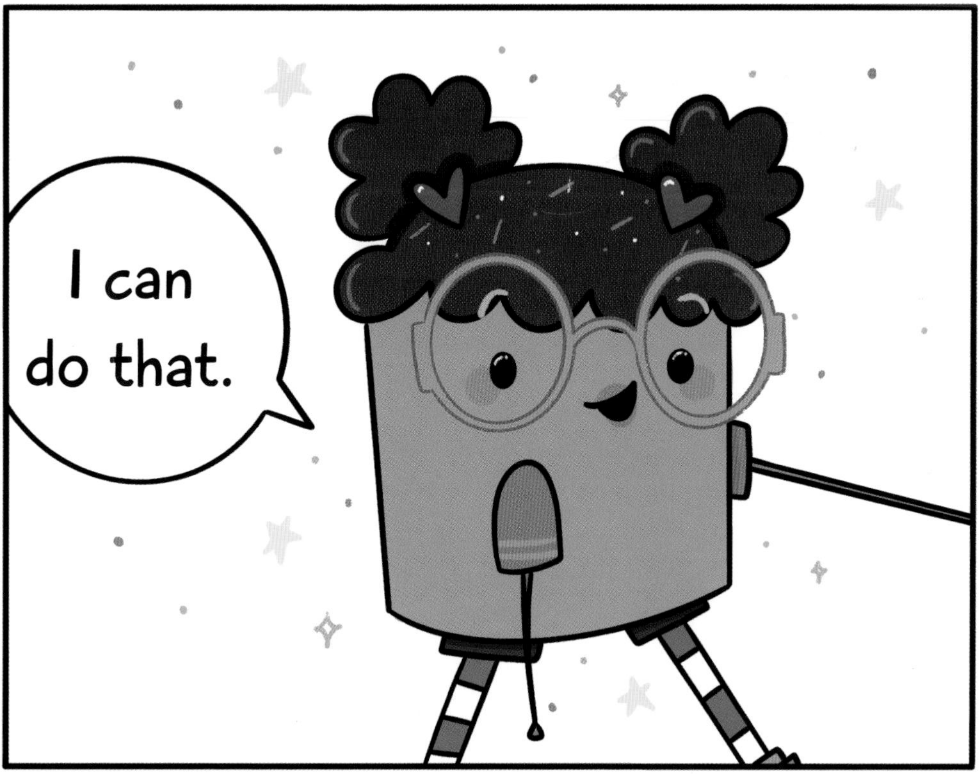
I can do that.

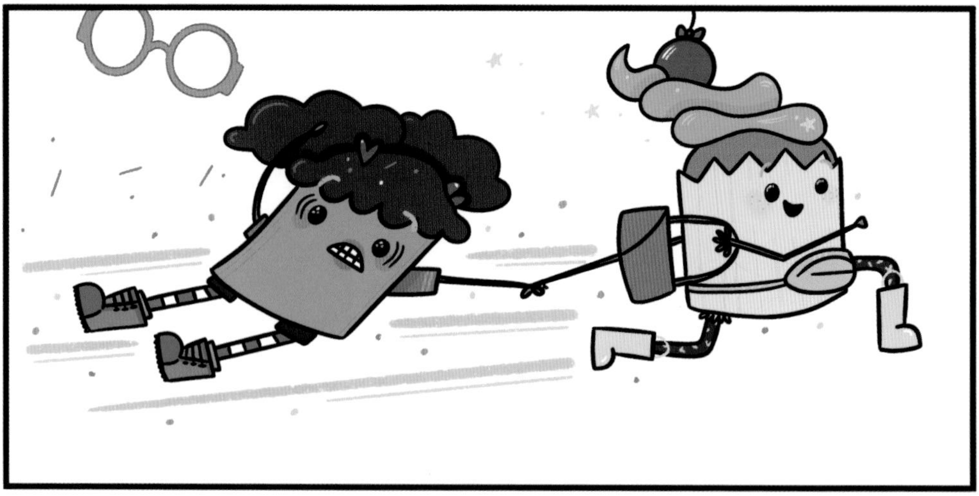

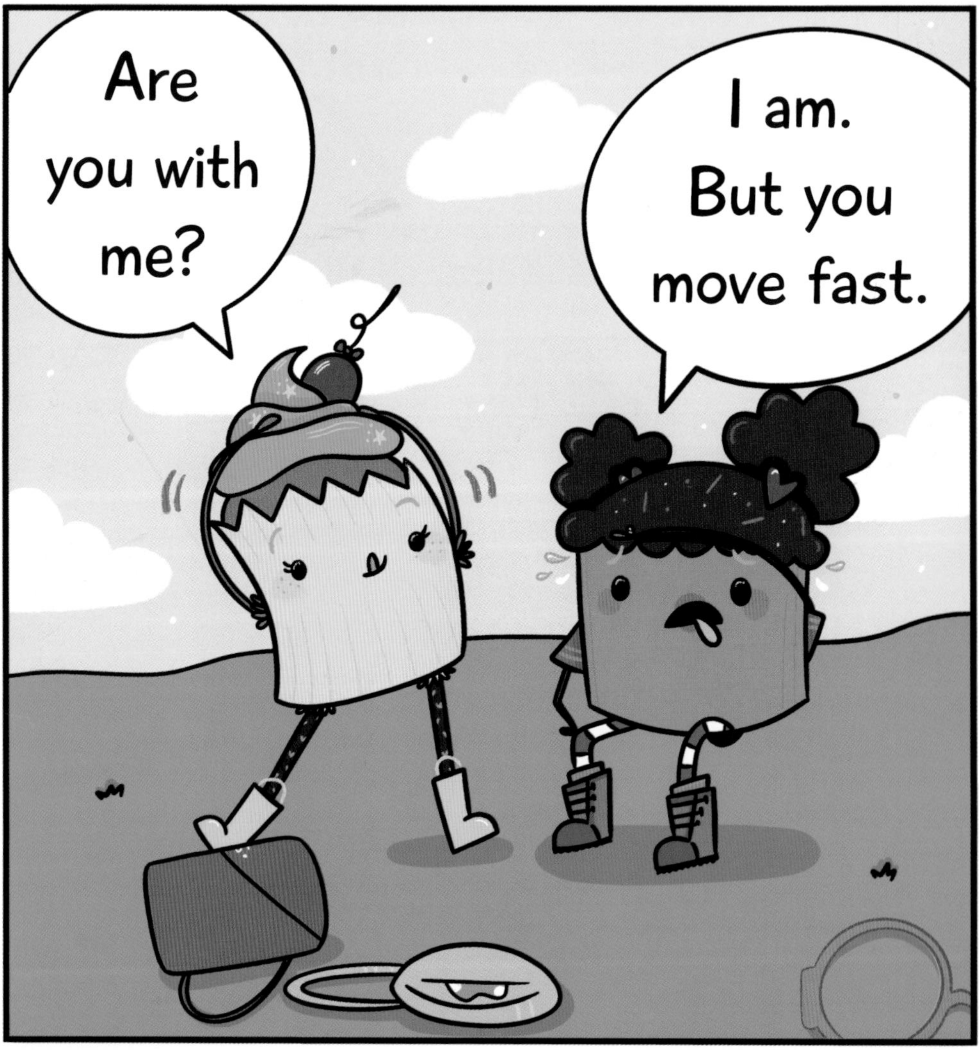
Are you with me?
I am. But you move fast.

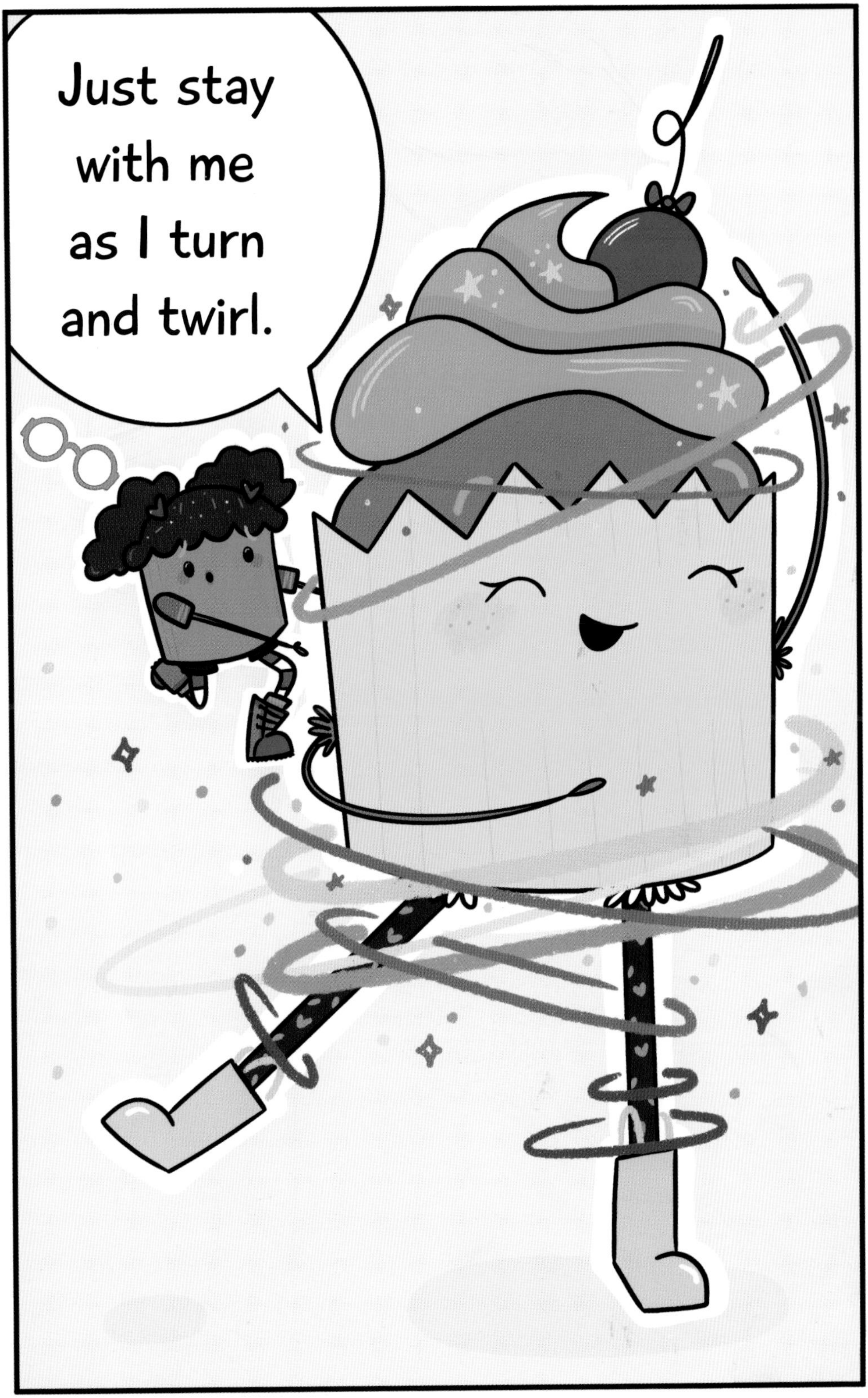
Just stay with me as I turn and twirl.

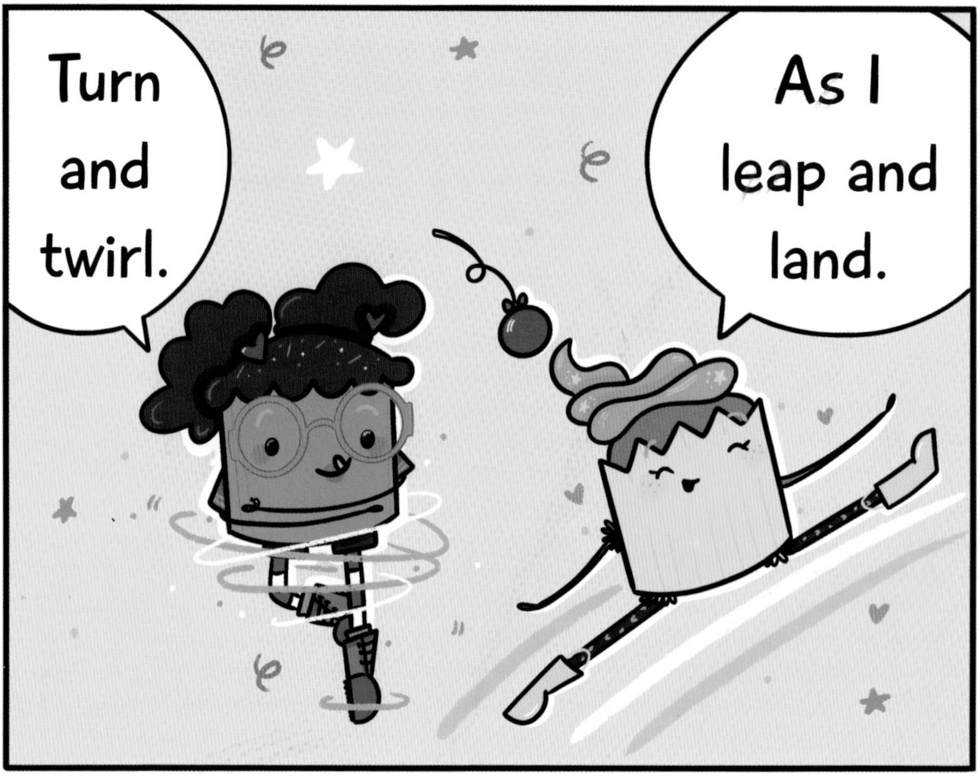
Turn and twirl.
As I leap and land.

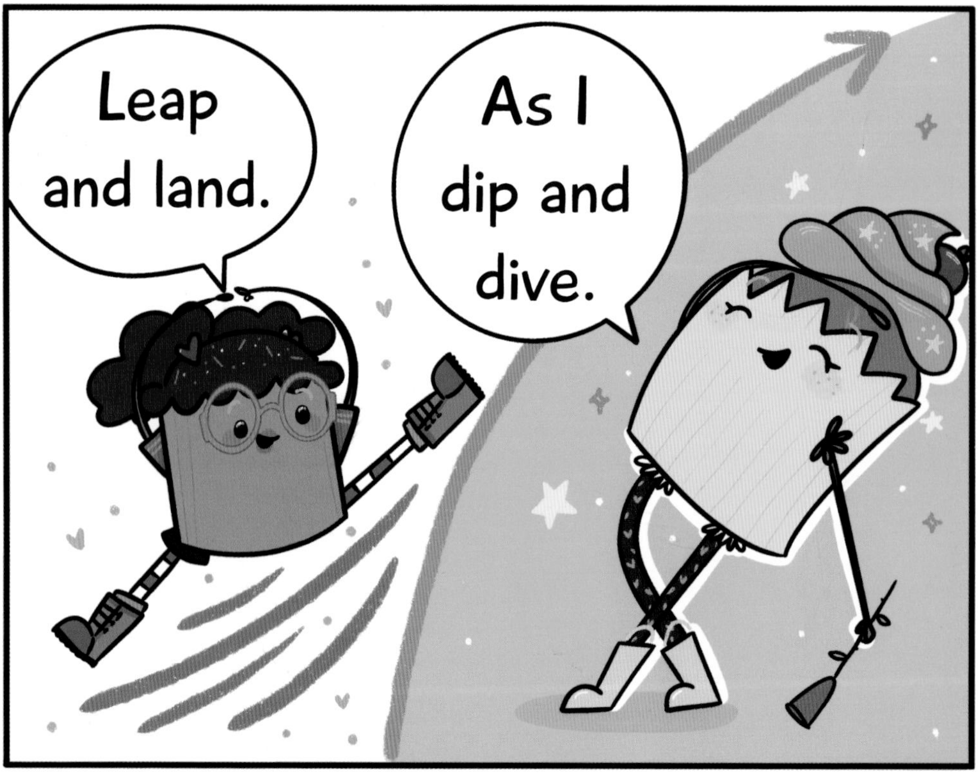
Leap and land.
As I dip and dive.

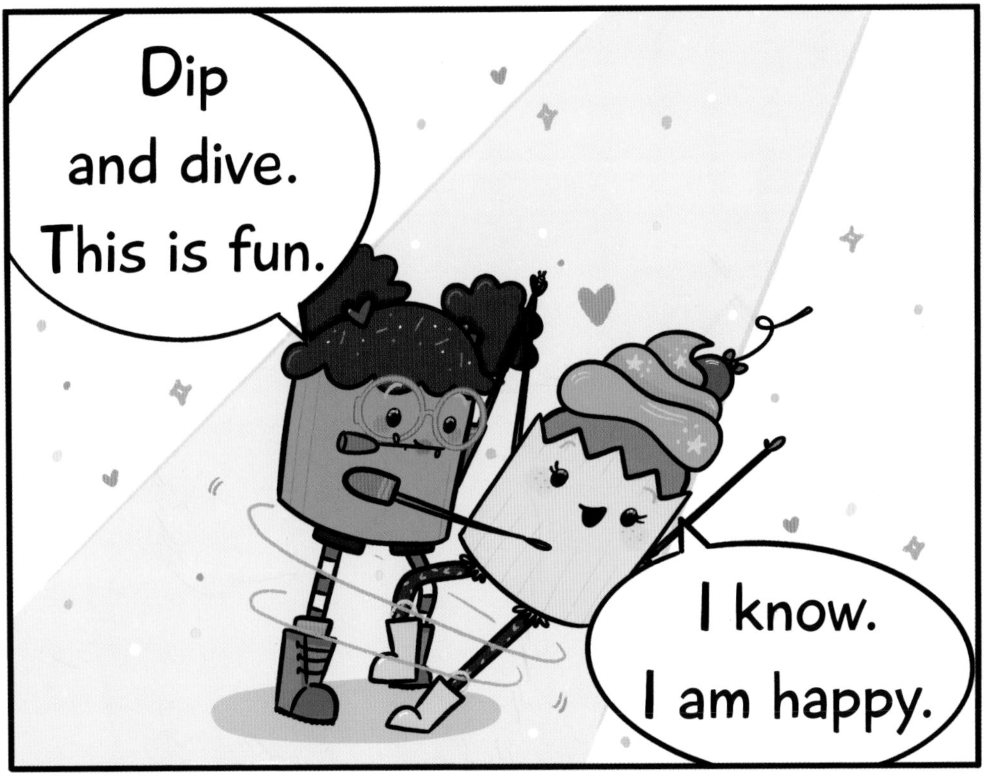
Dip and dive. This is fun.
I know. I am happy.

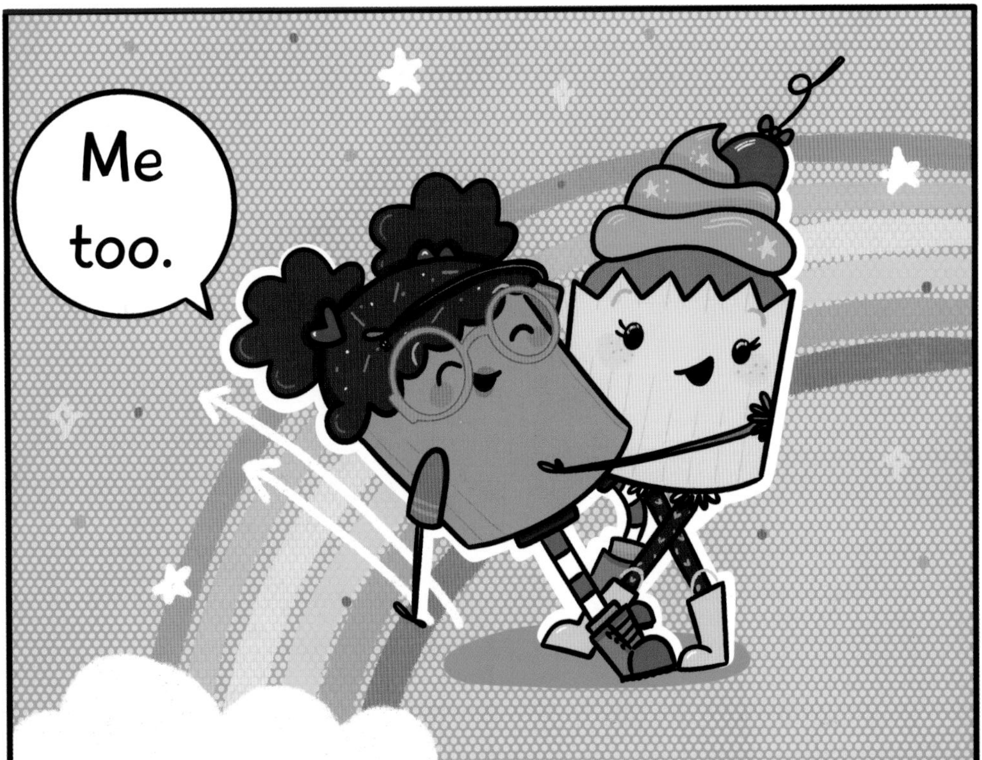
Me too.

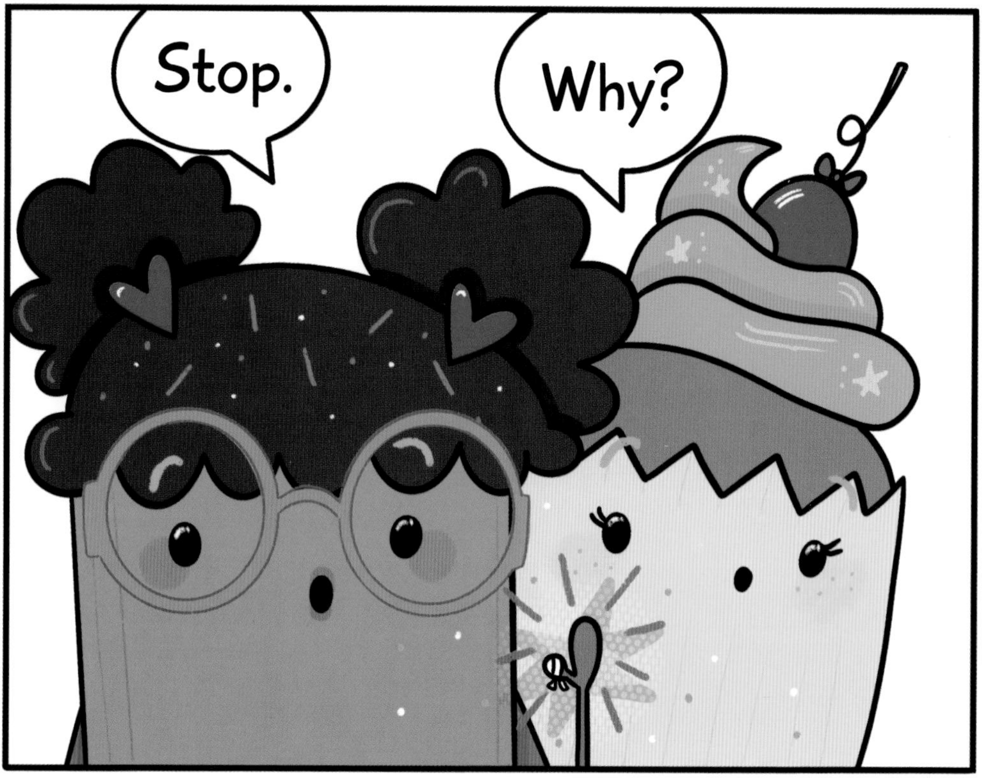
Stop.
Why?

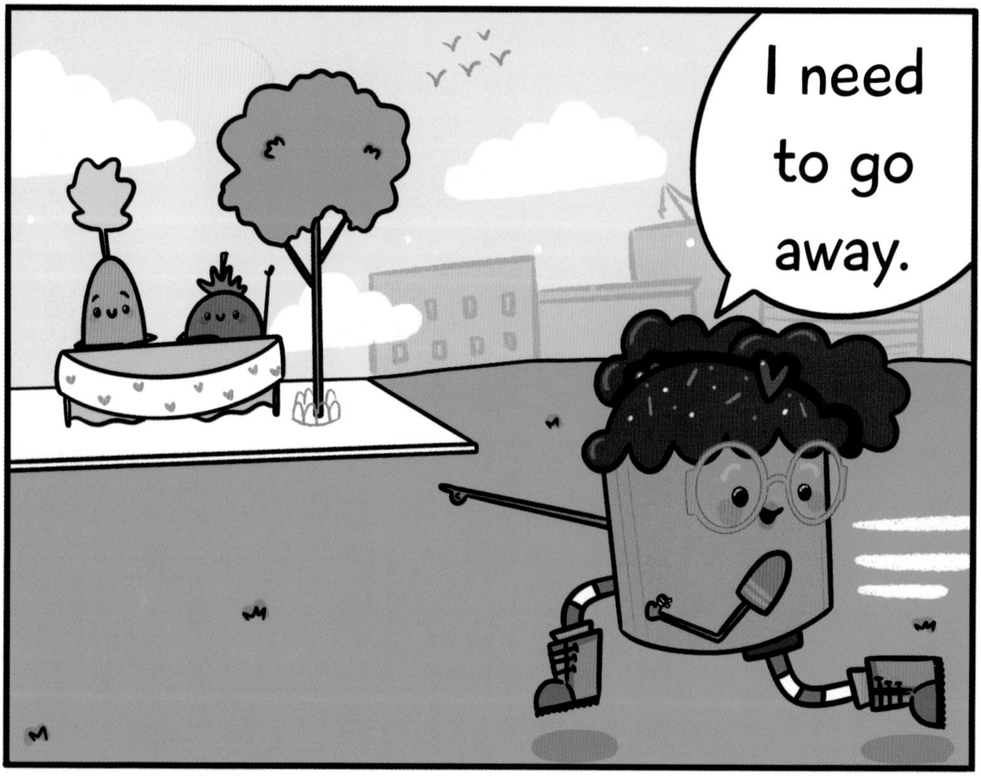
I need to go away.

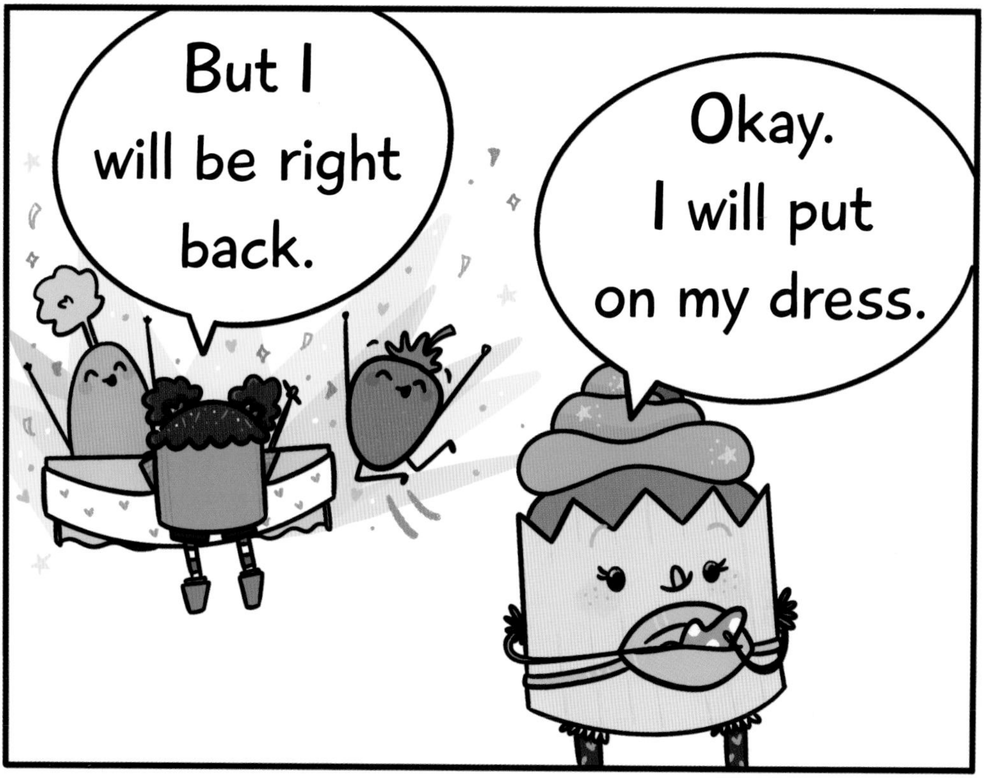
But I will be right back.
Okay. I will put on my dress.

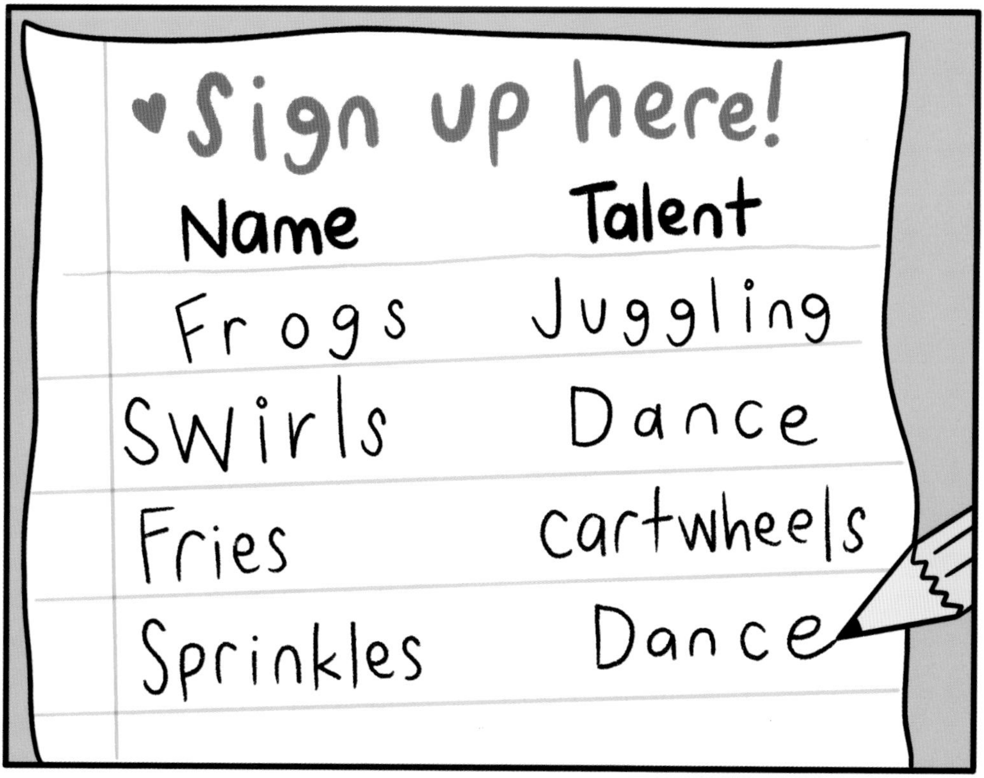
Sign up here!
Name Talent
Frogs Juggling
Swirls Dance
Fries cartwheels
Sprinkles Dance

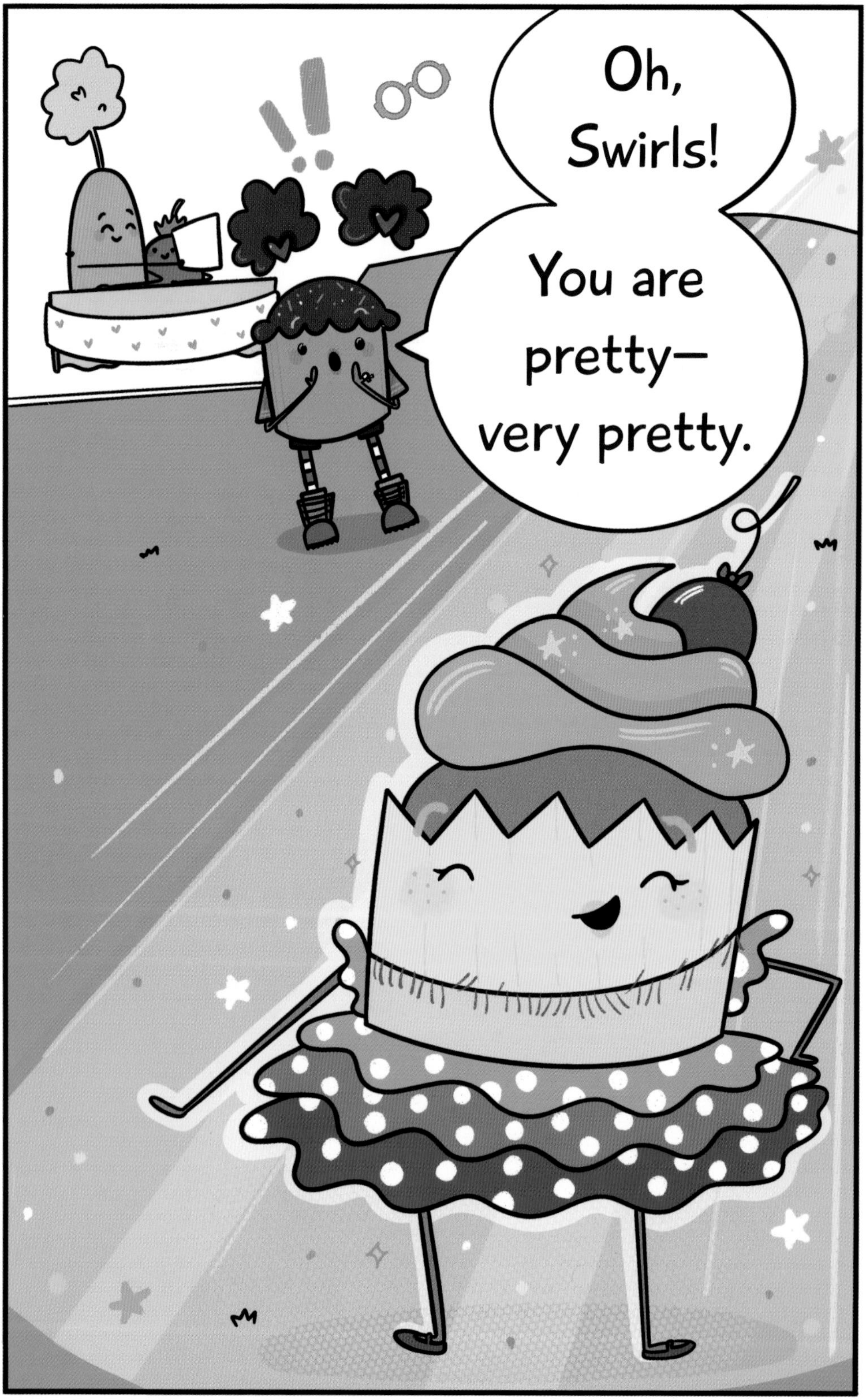
Oh, Swirls!
You are pretty— very pretty.

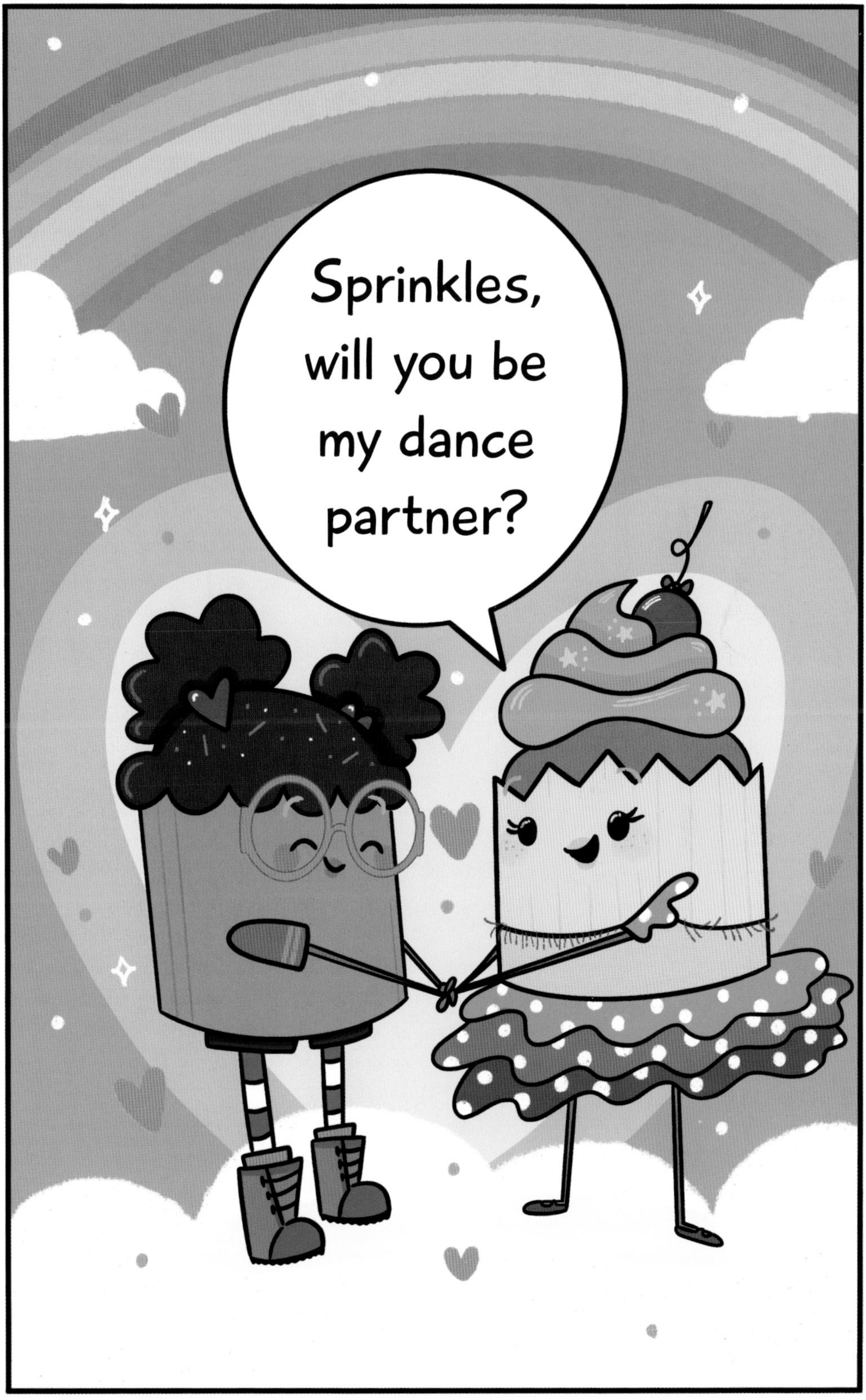
Sprinkles, will you be my dance partner?

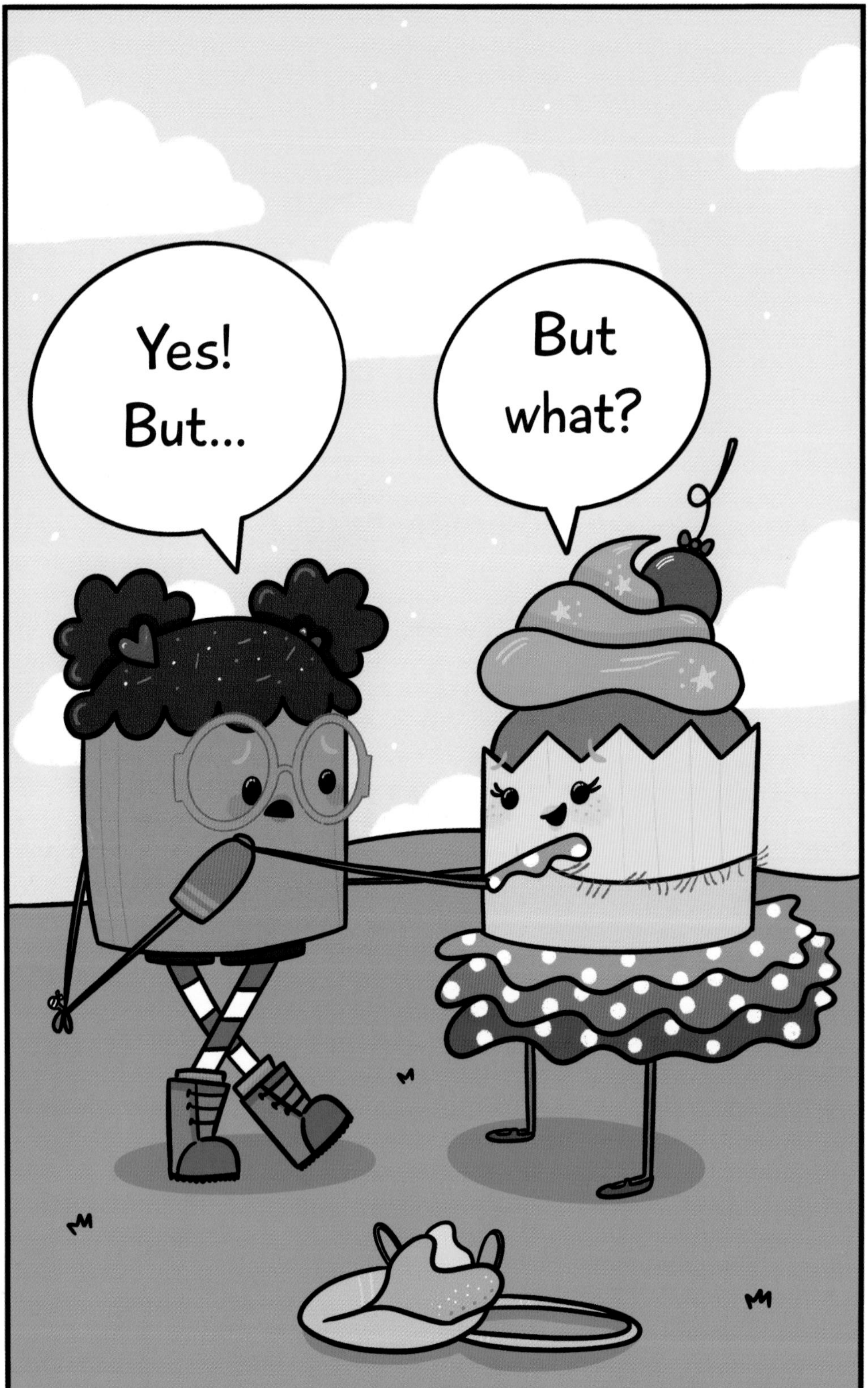
Yes! But...
But what?

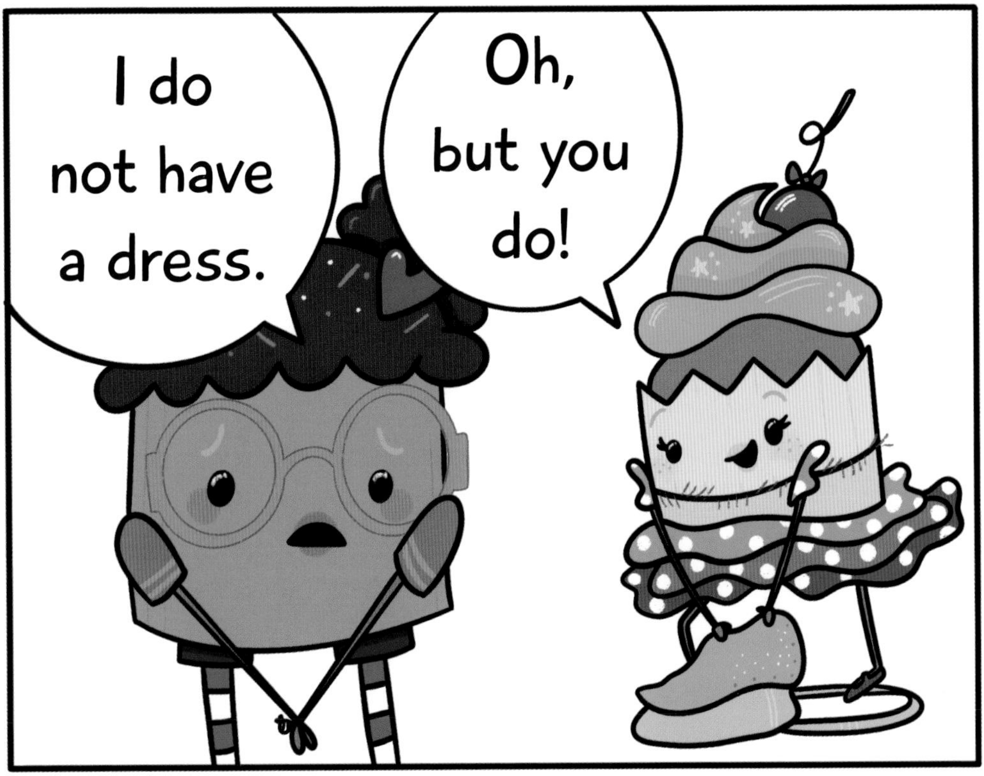
I do not have a dress.
Oh, but you do!

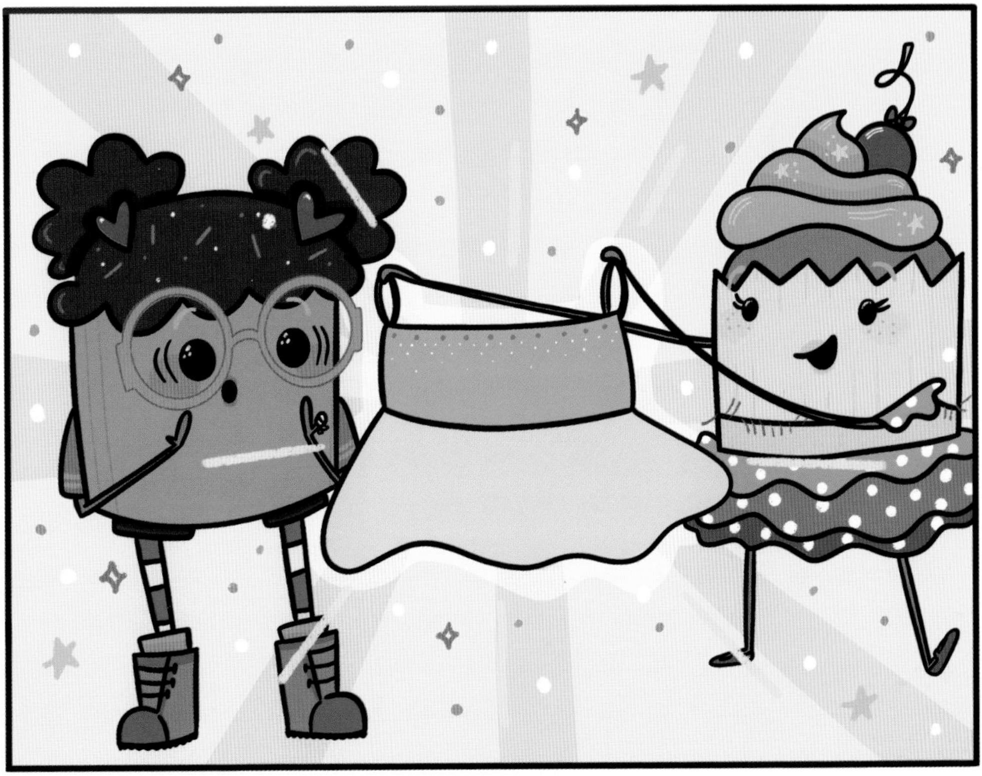

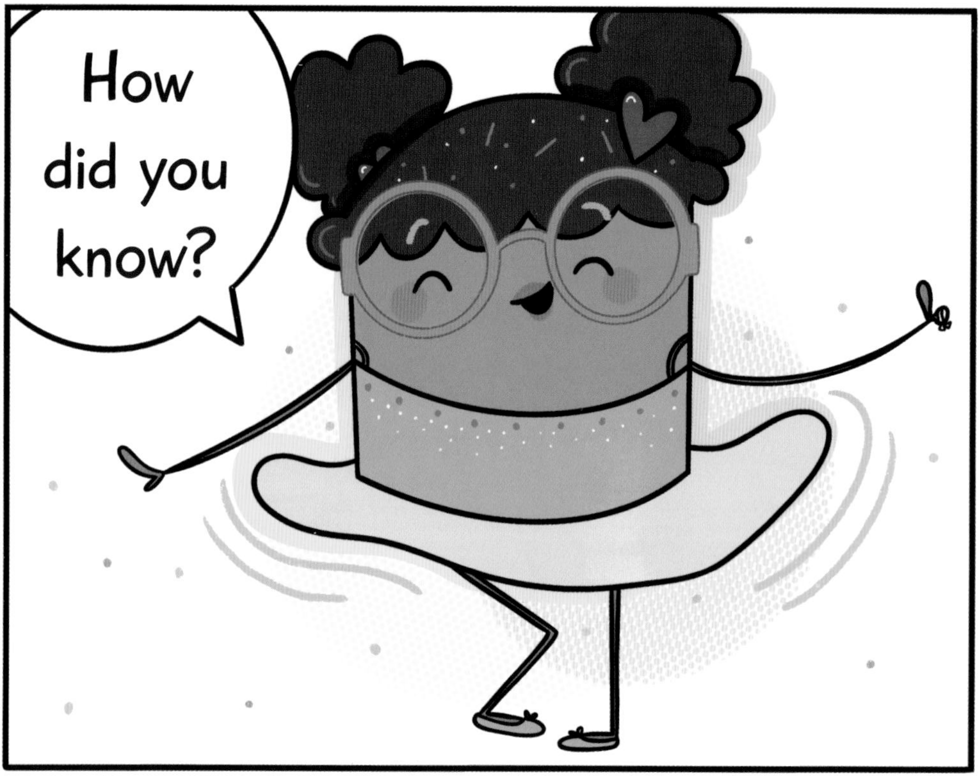
How did you know?

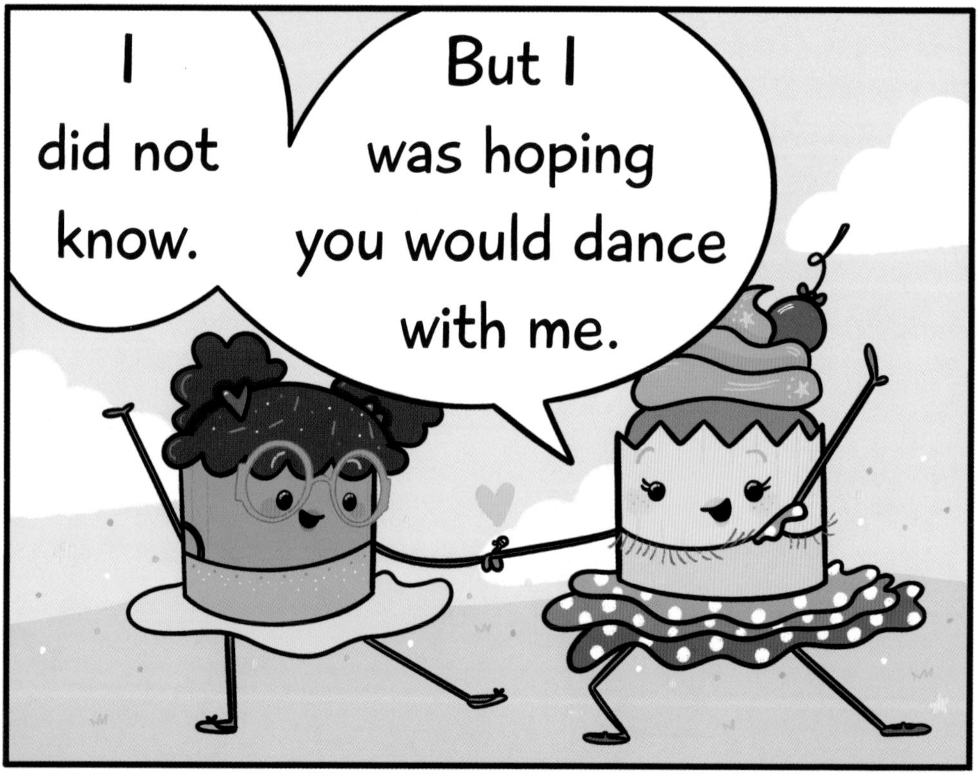
I did not know.
But I was hoping you would dance with me.

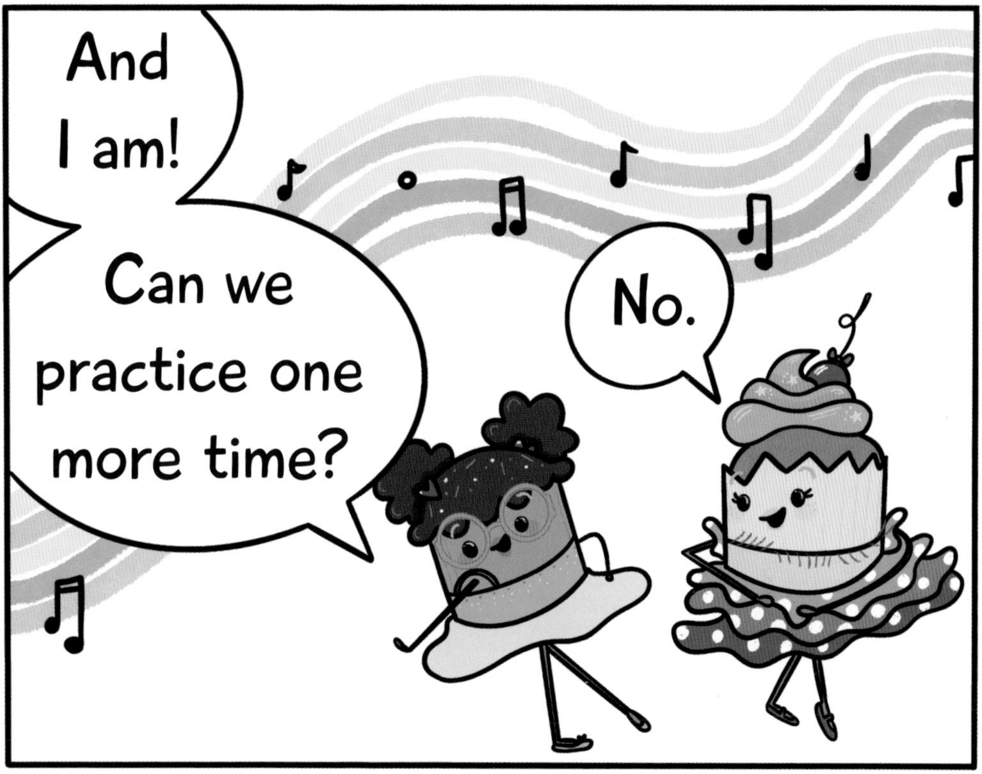
And I am!
Can we practice one more time?
No.

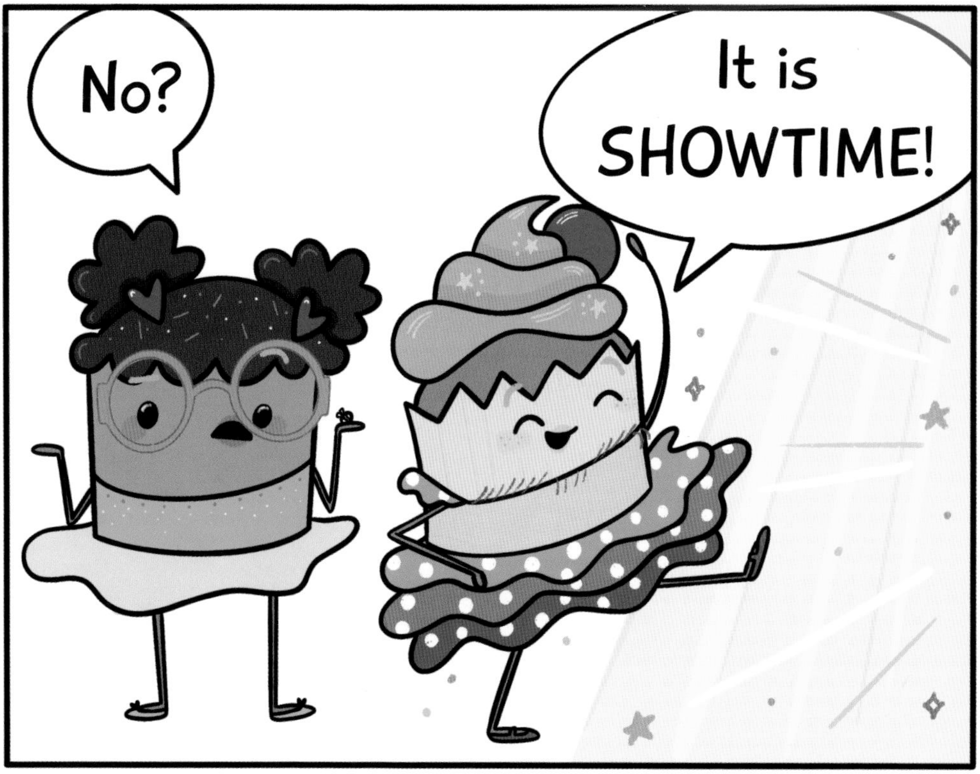
No?
It is SHOWTIME!

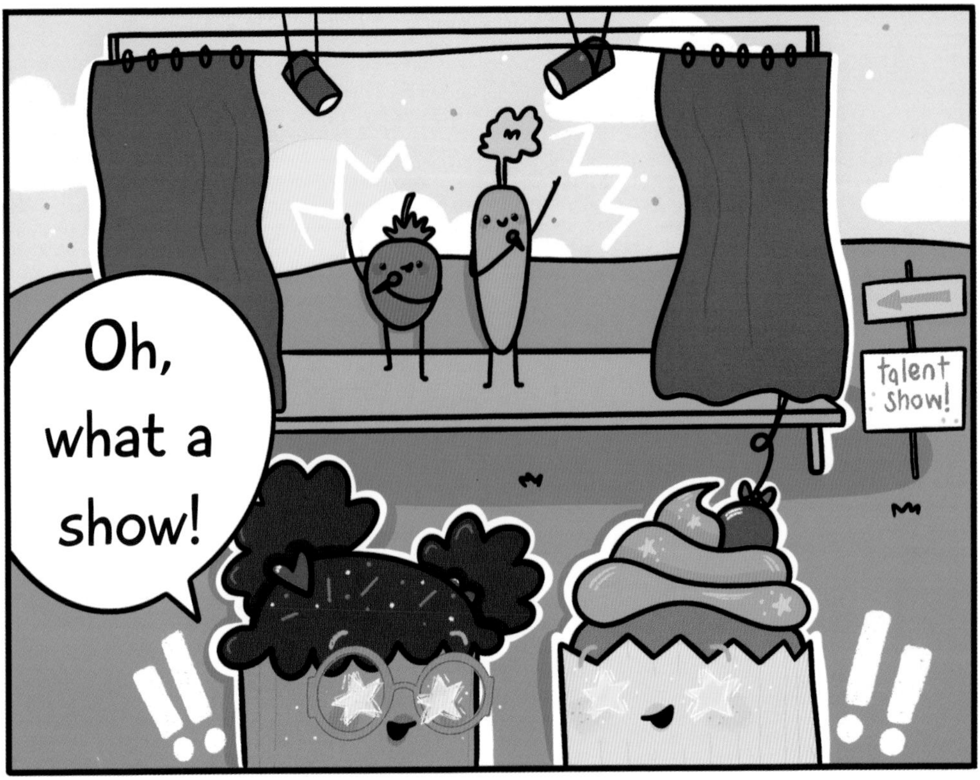
Oh, what a show!
talent show!

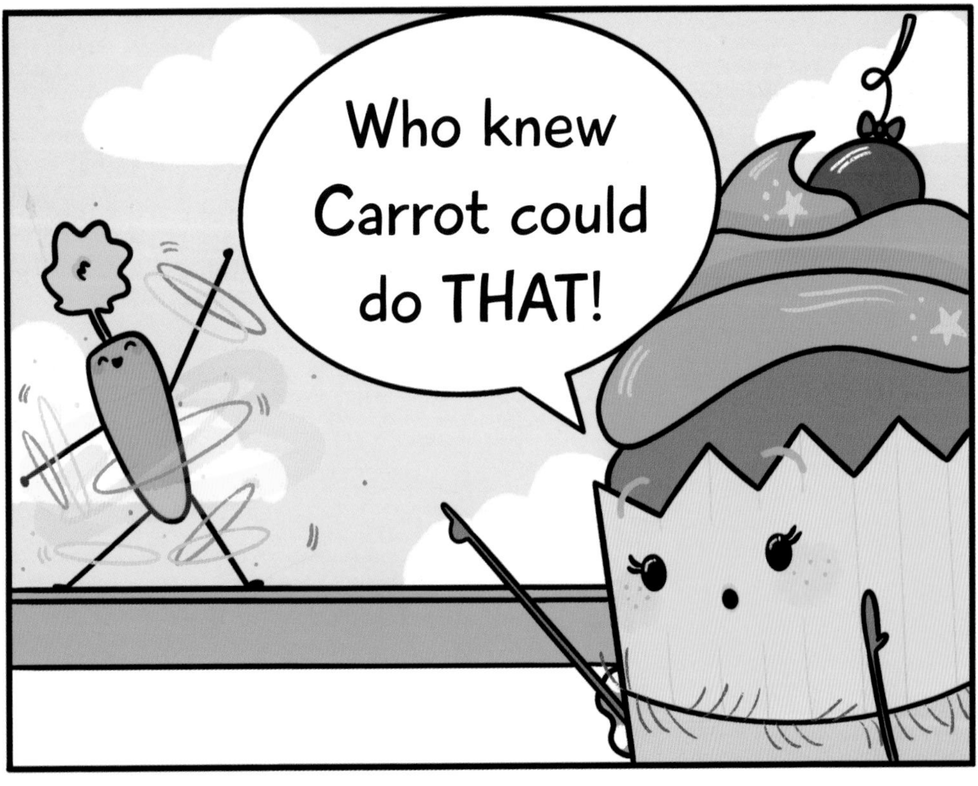
Who knew Carrot could do THAT!

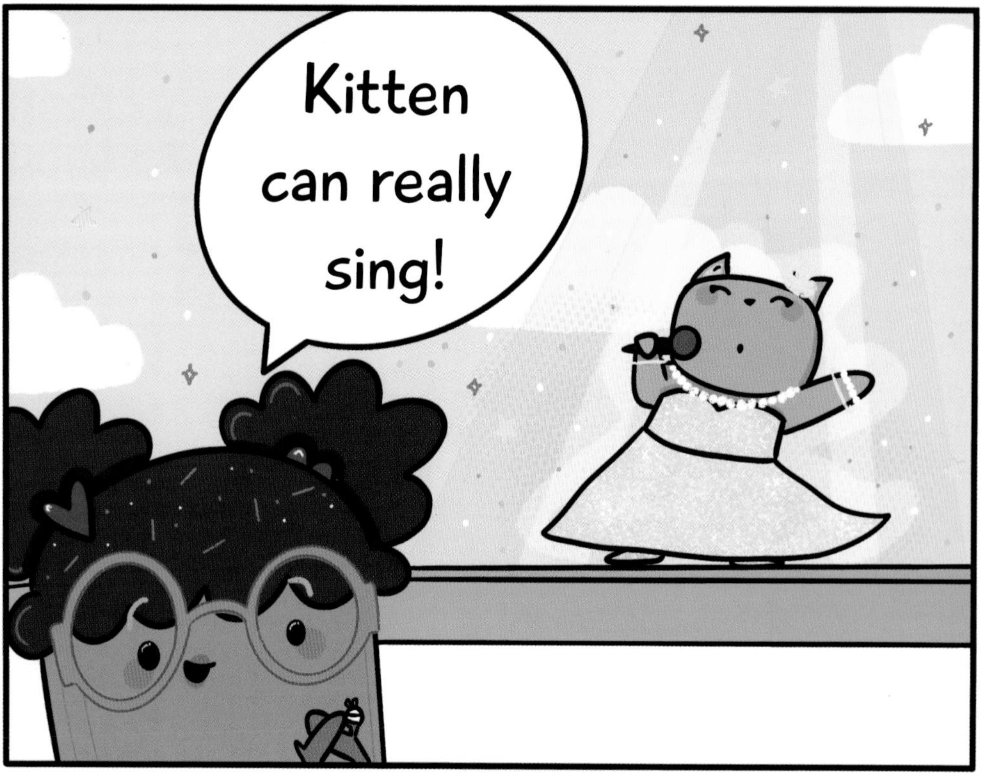
Kitten can really sing!

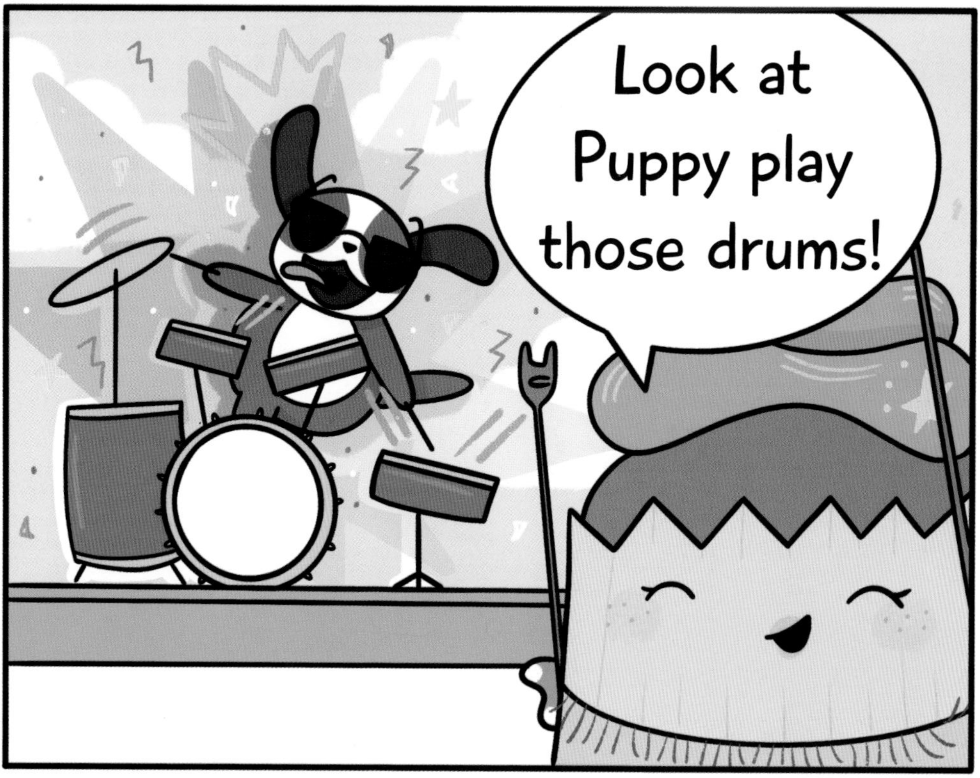
Look at Puppy play those drums!

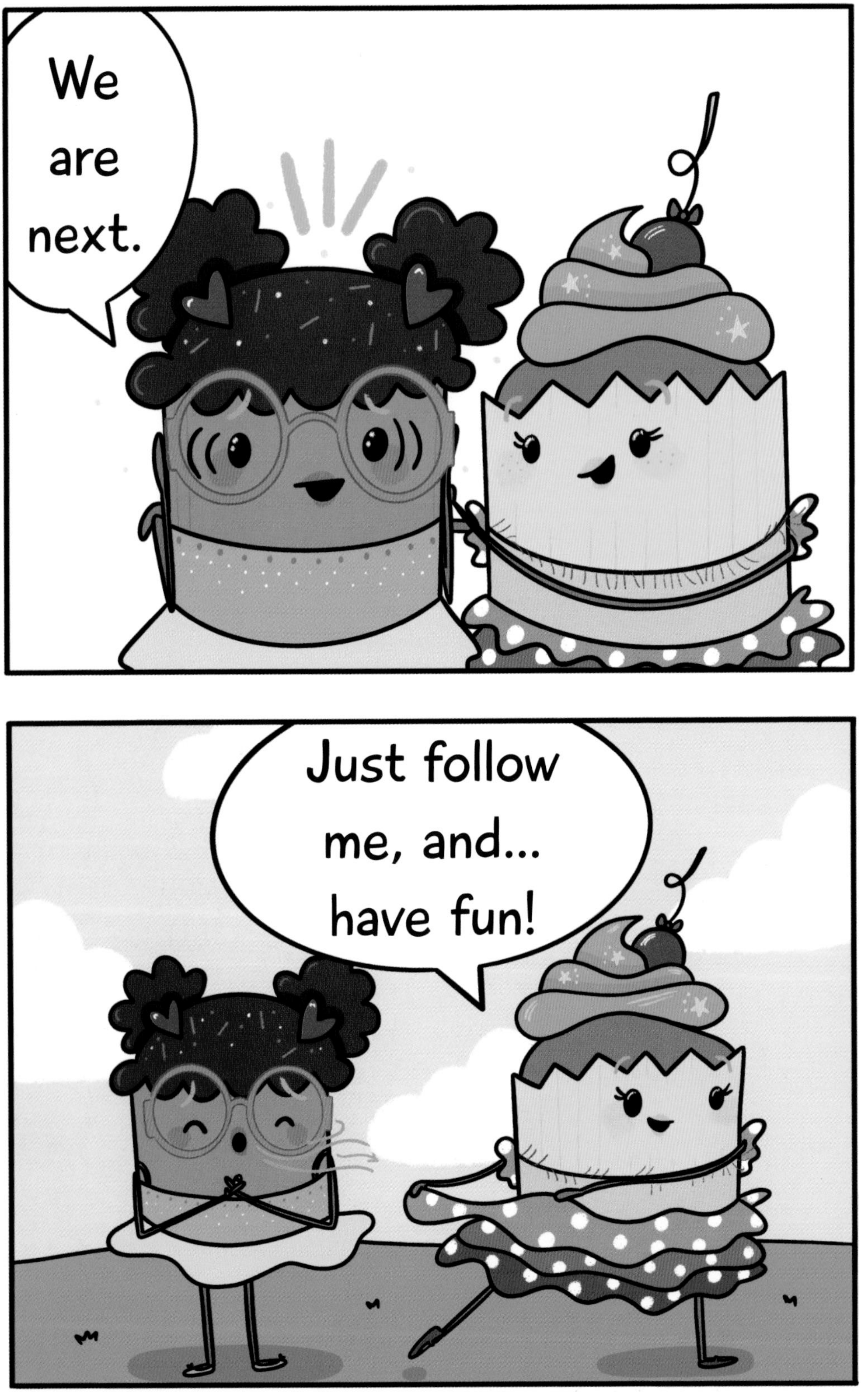
We are next.
Just follow me, and... have fun!

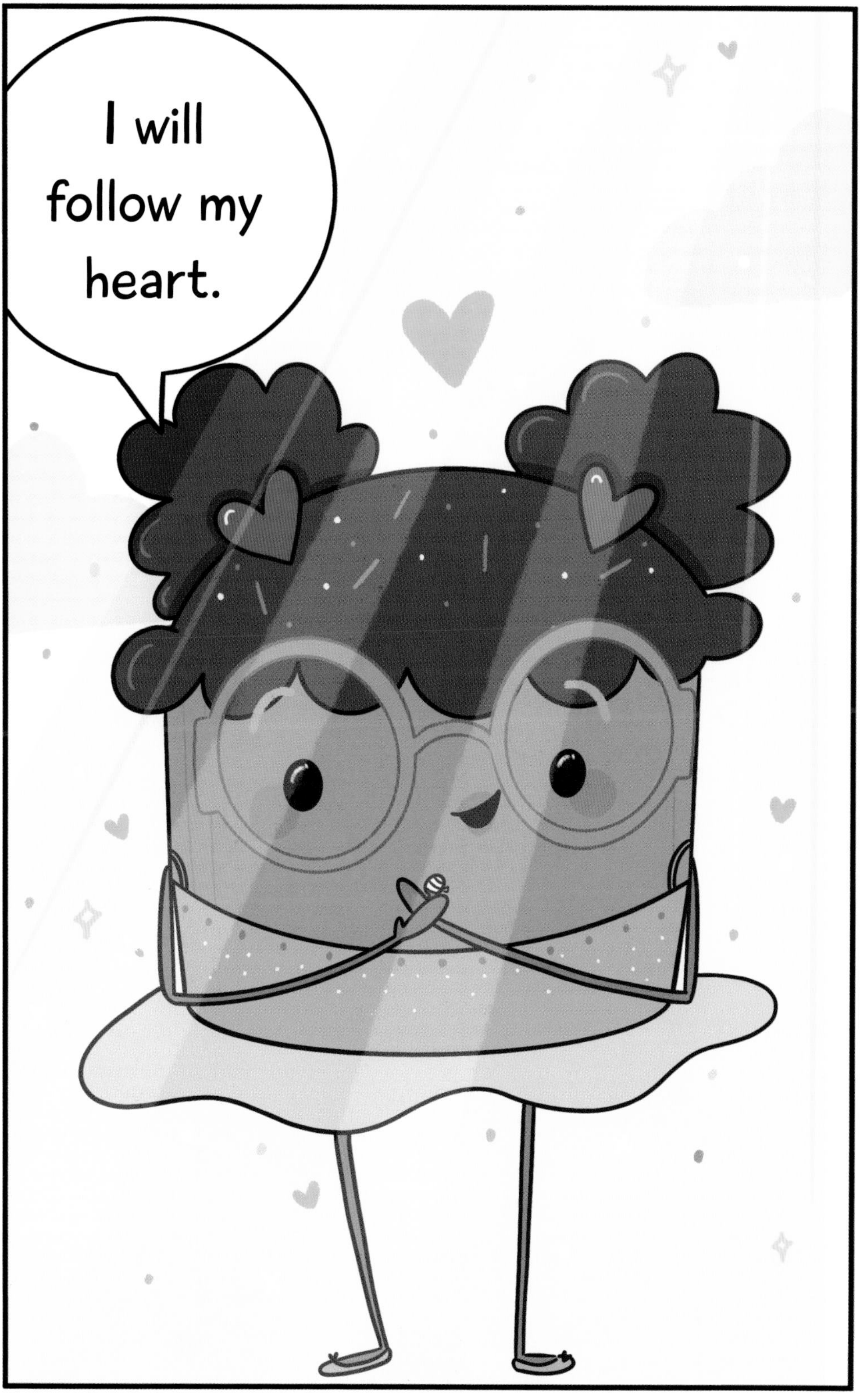
I will follow my heart.

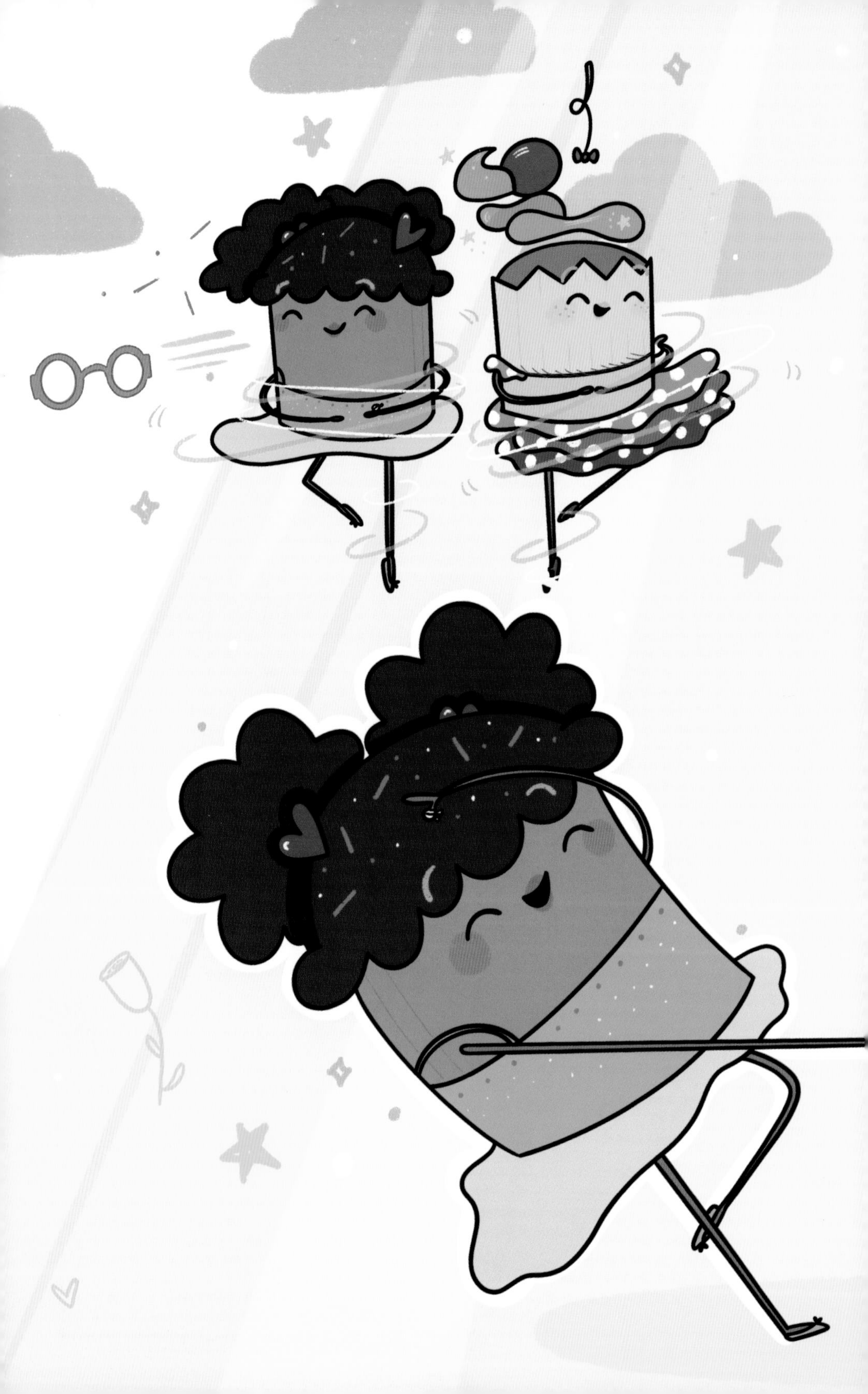

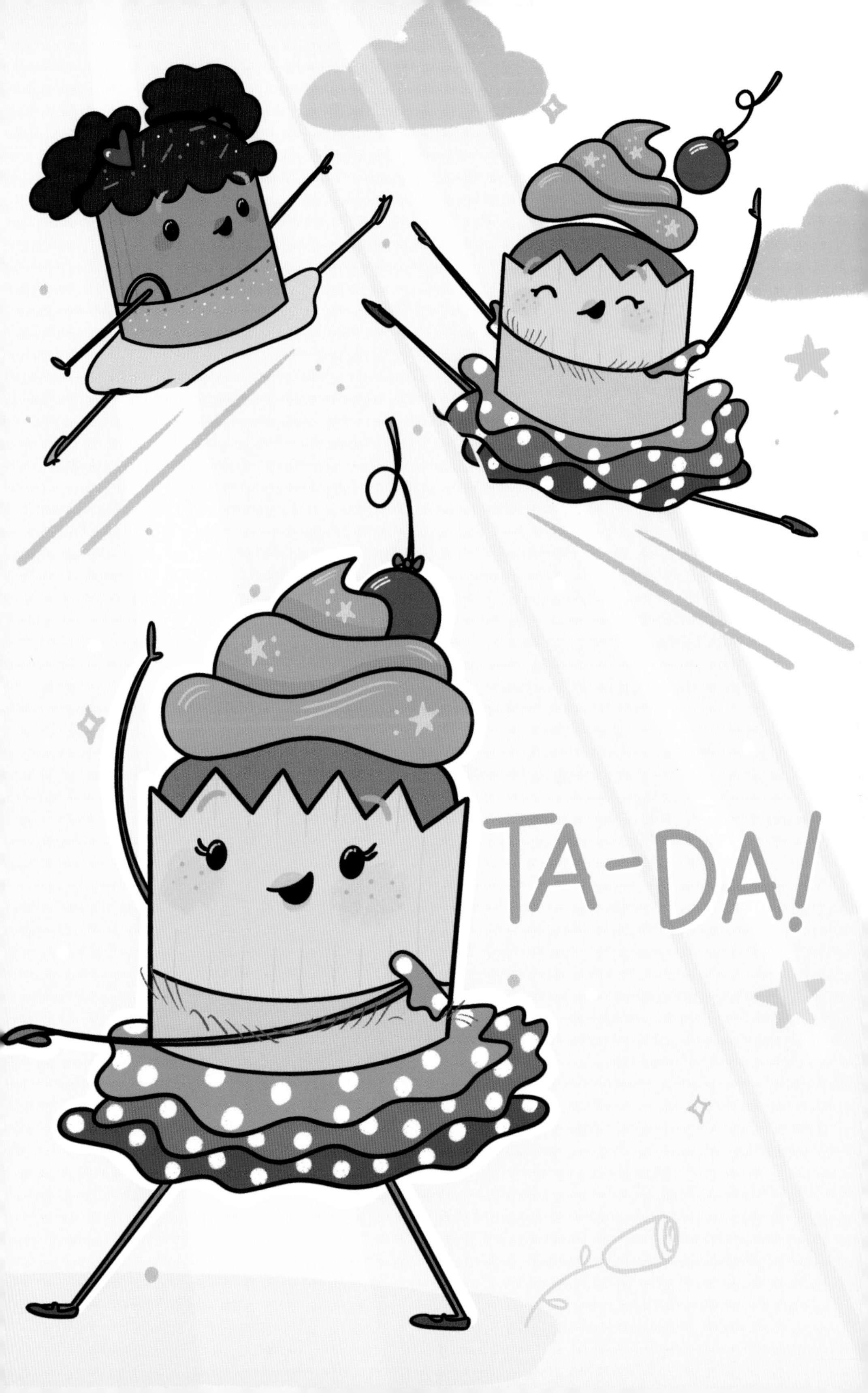
TA-DA!

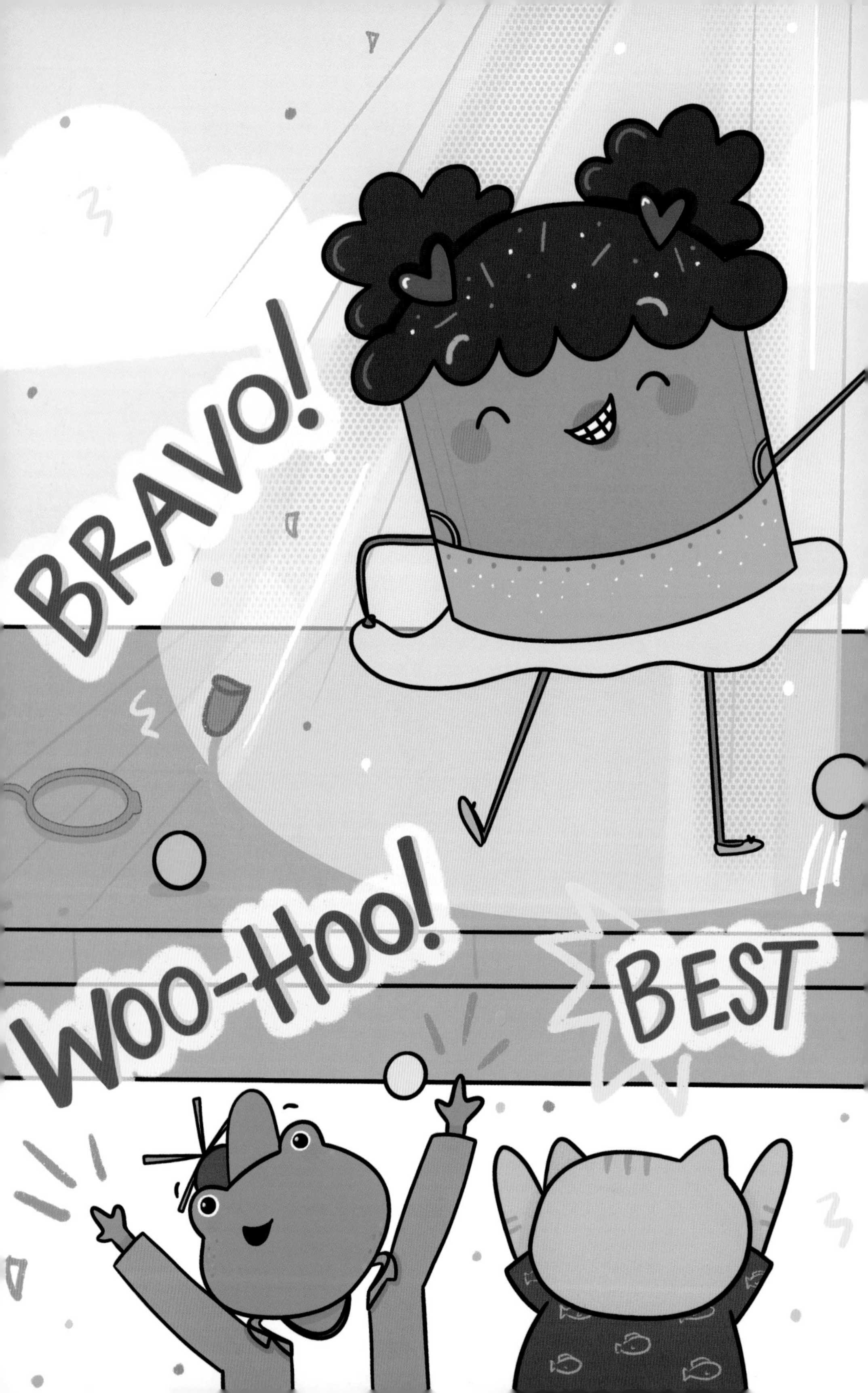
BRAVO!
WOO-HOO!
BEST

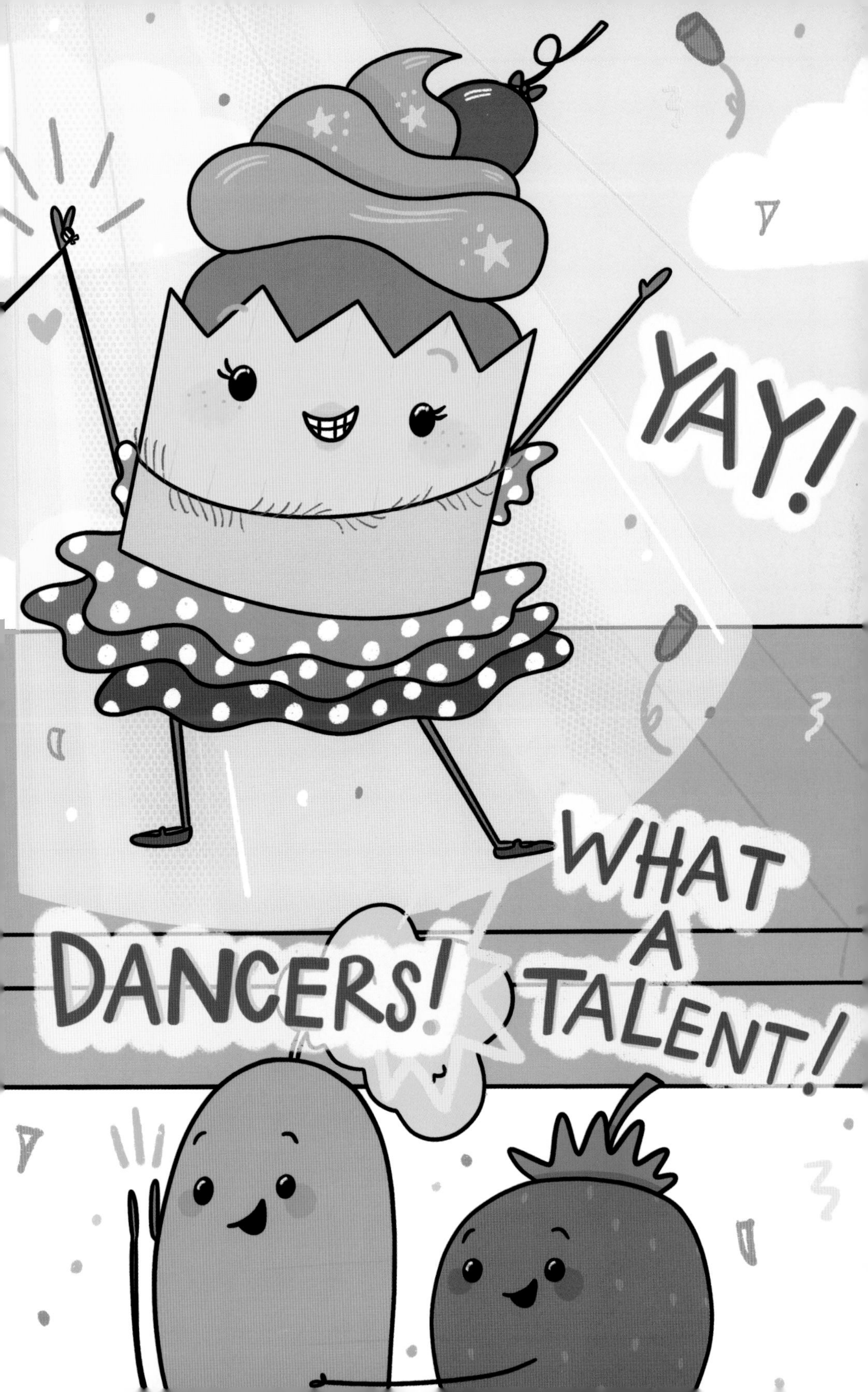
YAY!
WHAT A TALENT!
DANCERS!

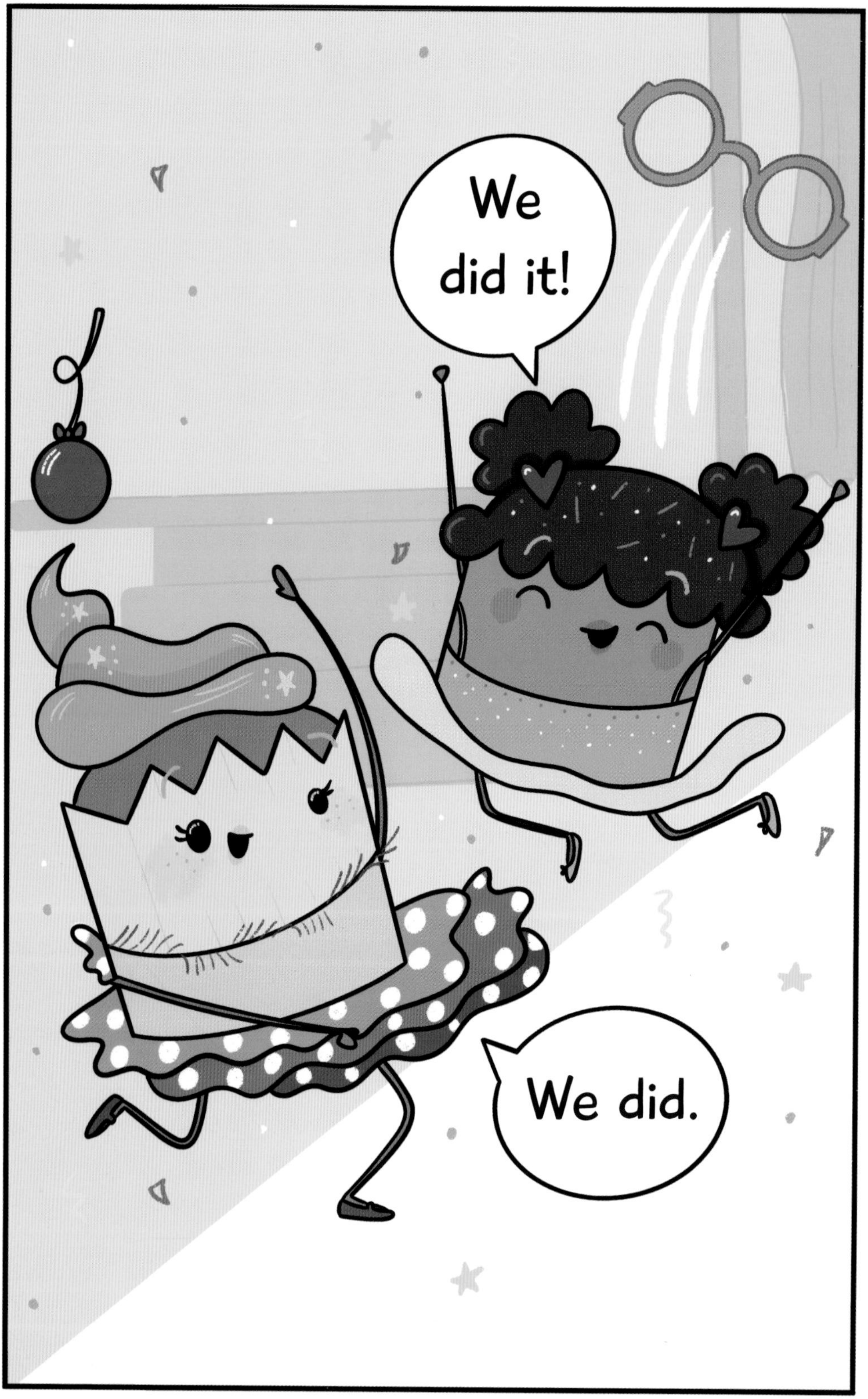
We did it!
We did.

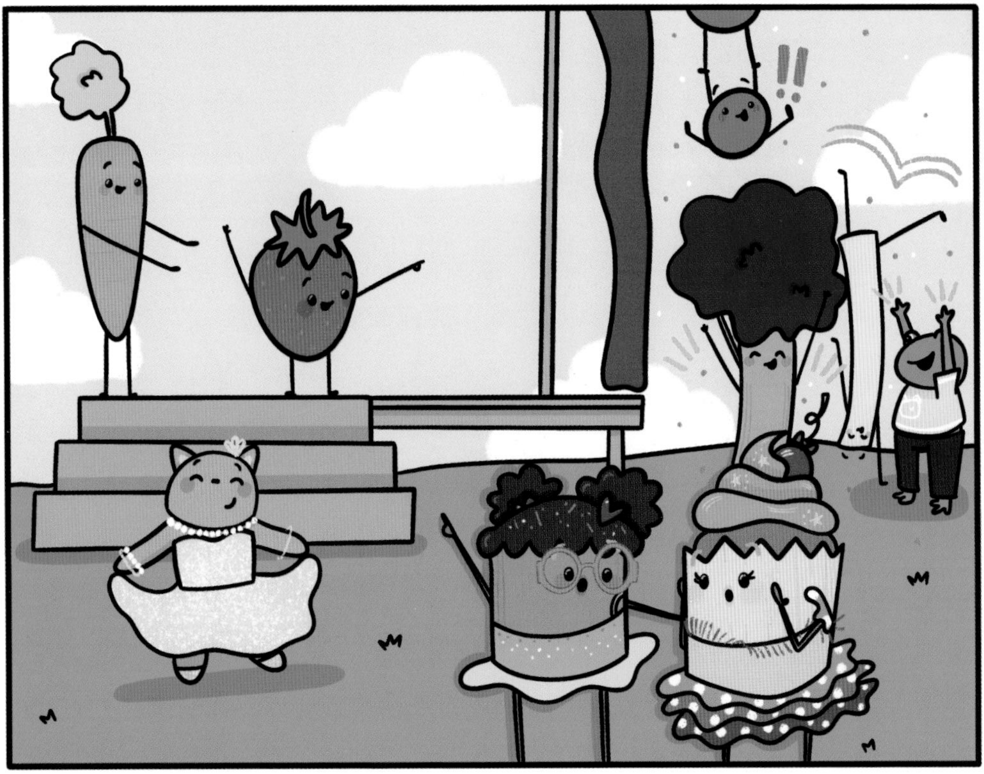

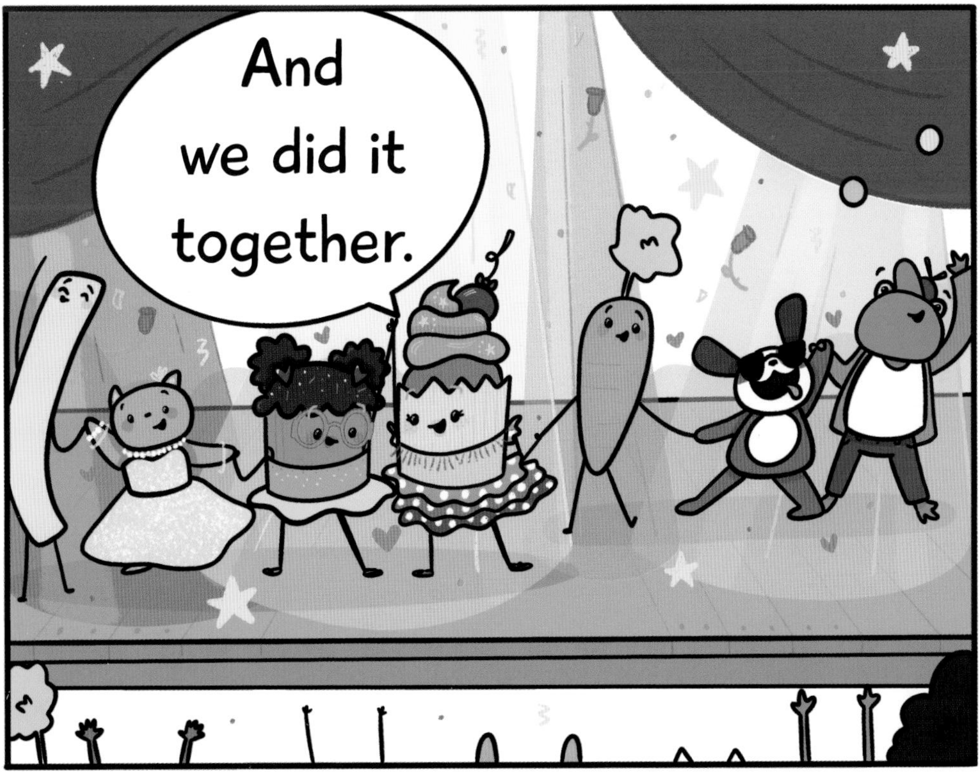
And we did it together.

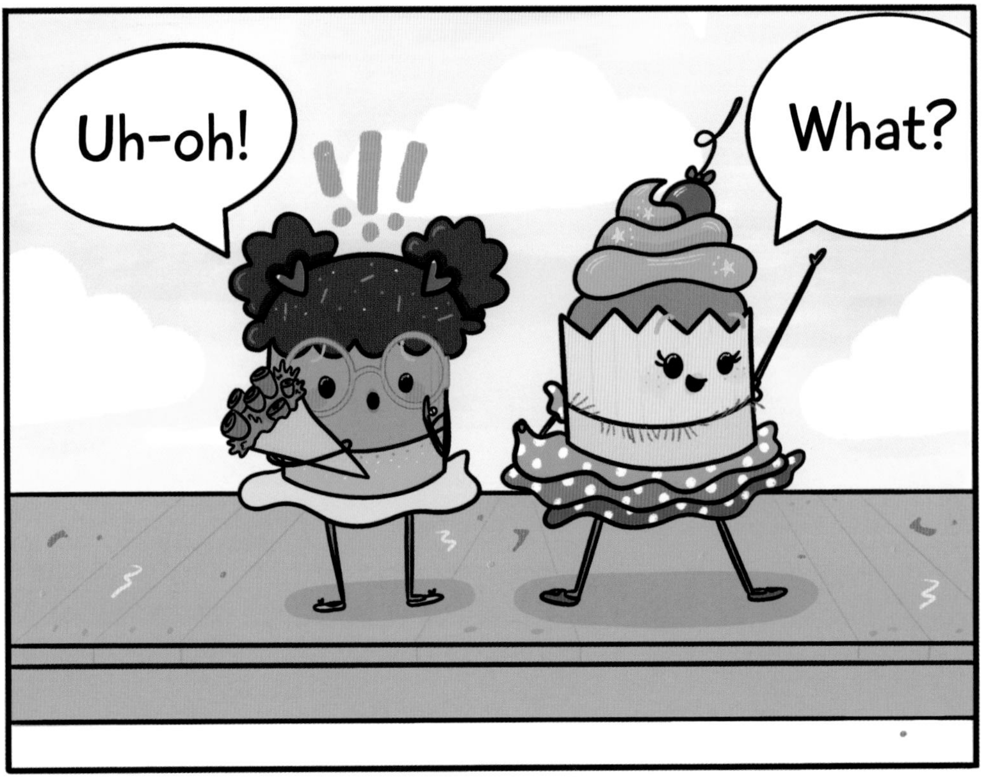
Uh-oh!
What?

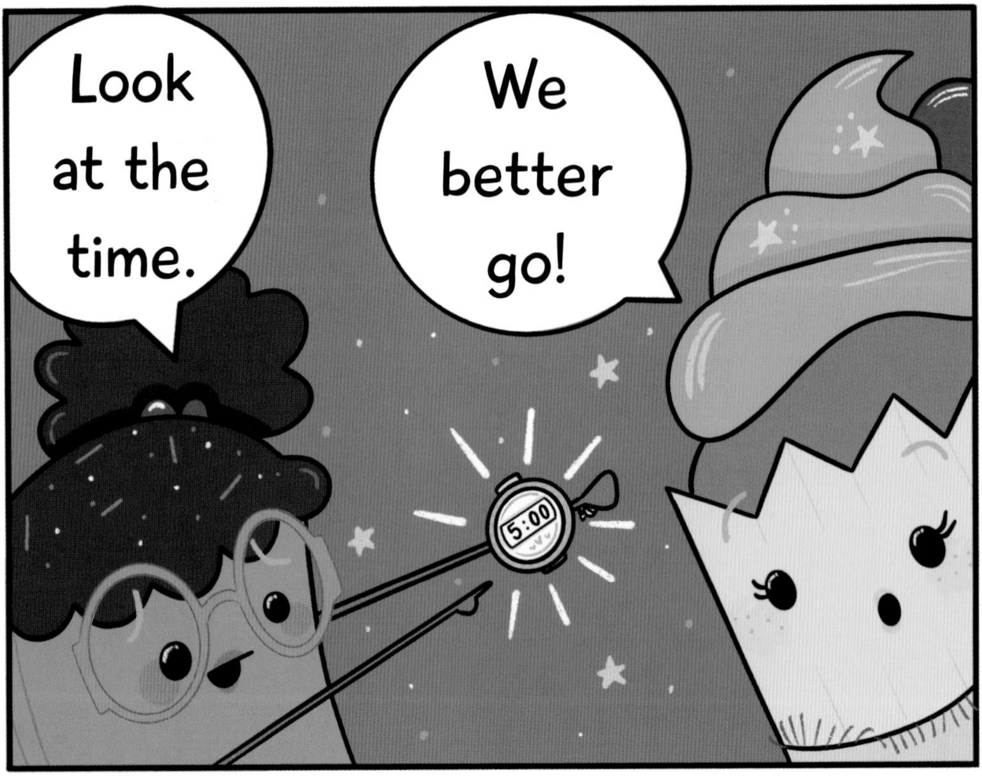
Look at the time.
We better go!
5:00

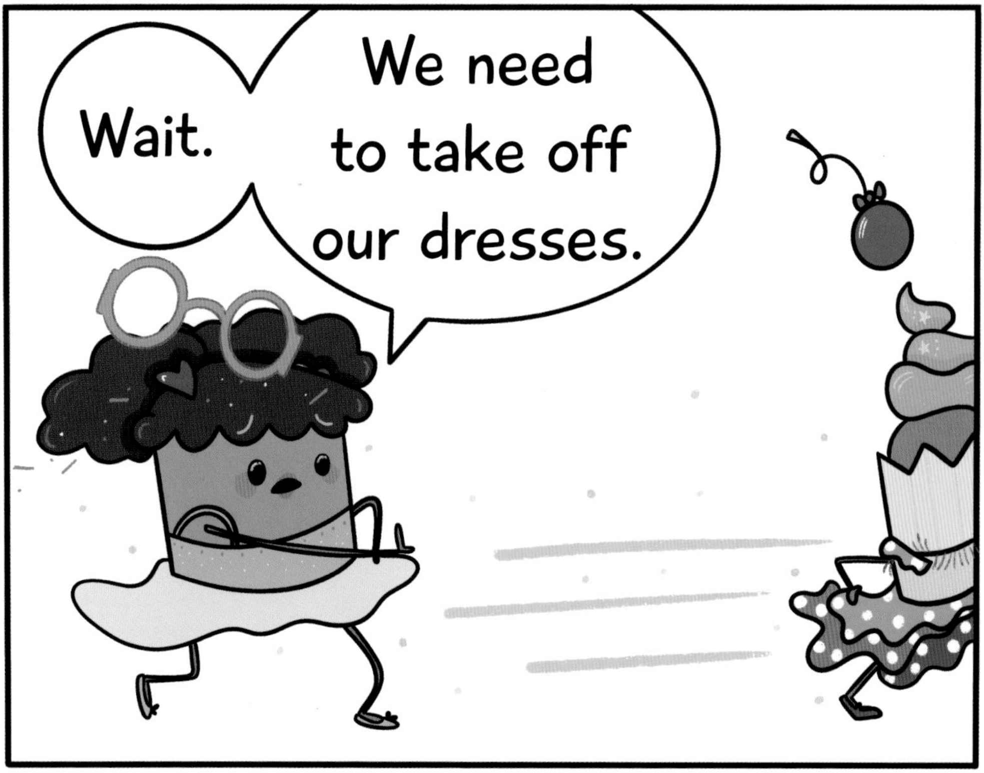
Wait.
We need to take off our dresses.

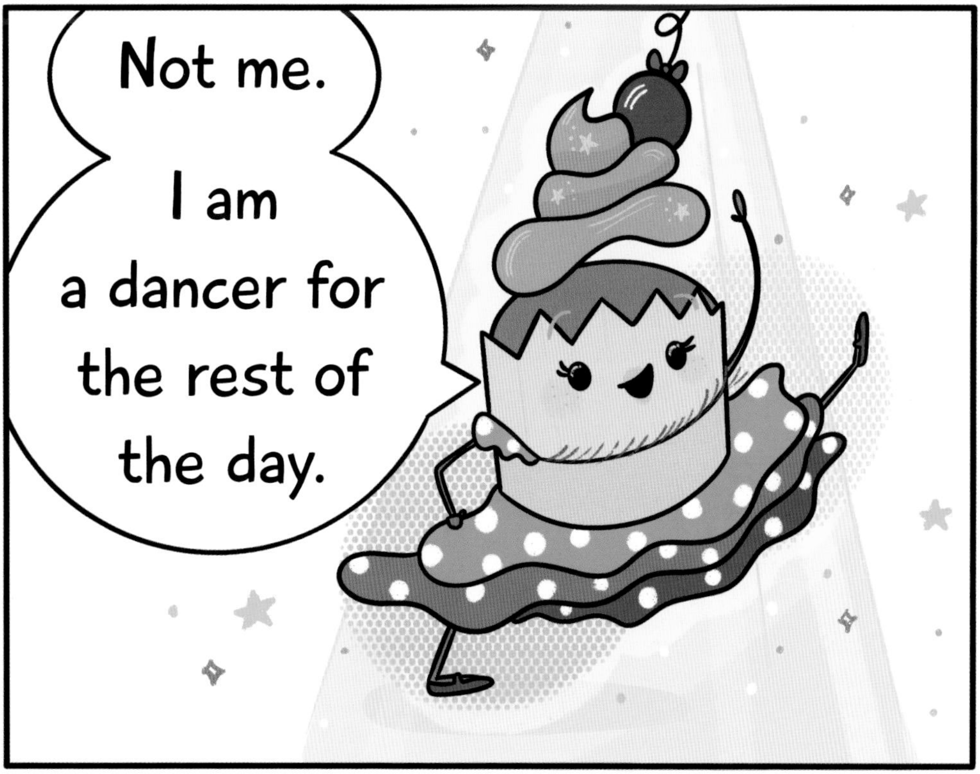
Not me.
I am a dancer for the rest of the day.

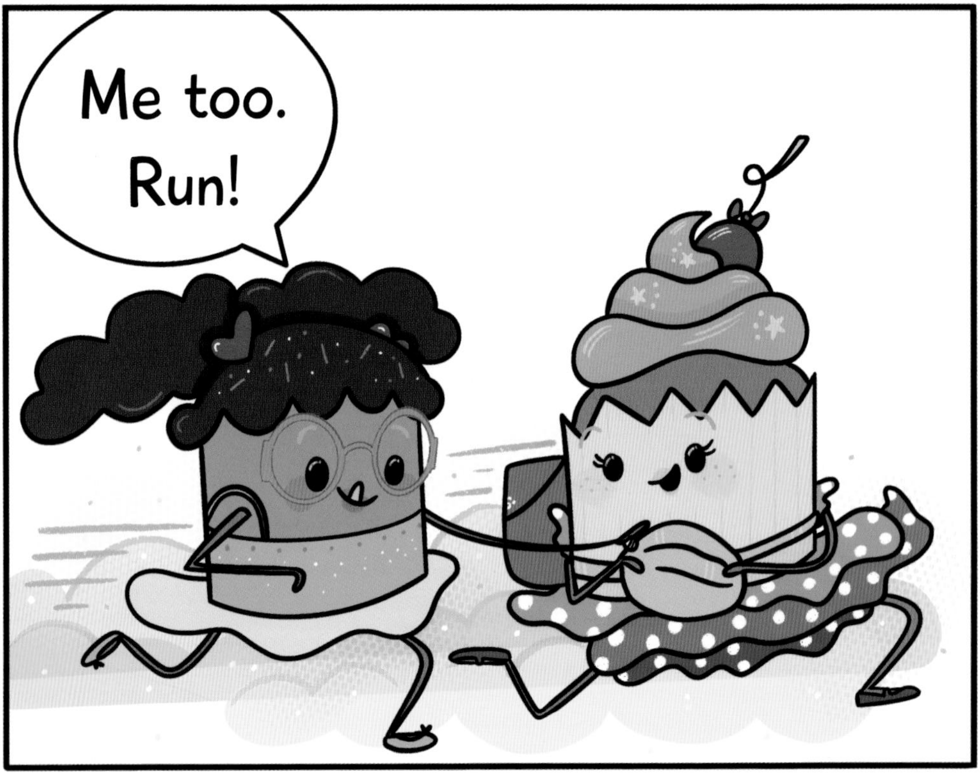
Me too. Run!

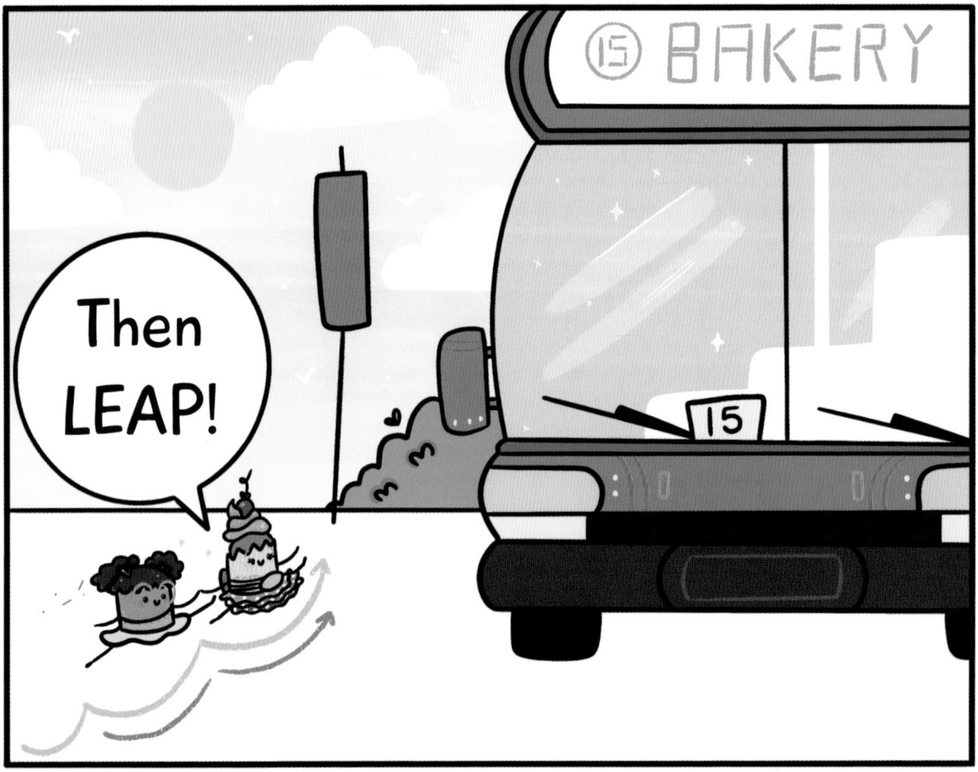
15 BAKERY
Then LEAP!
15

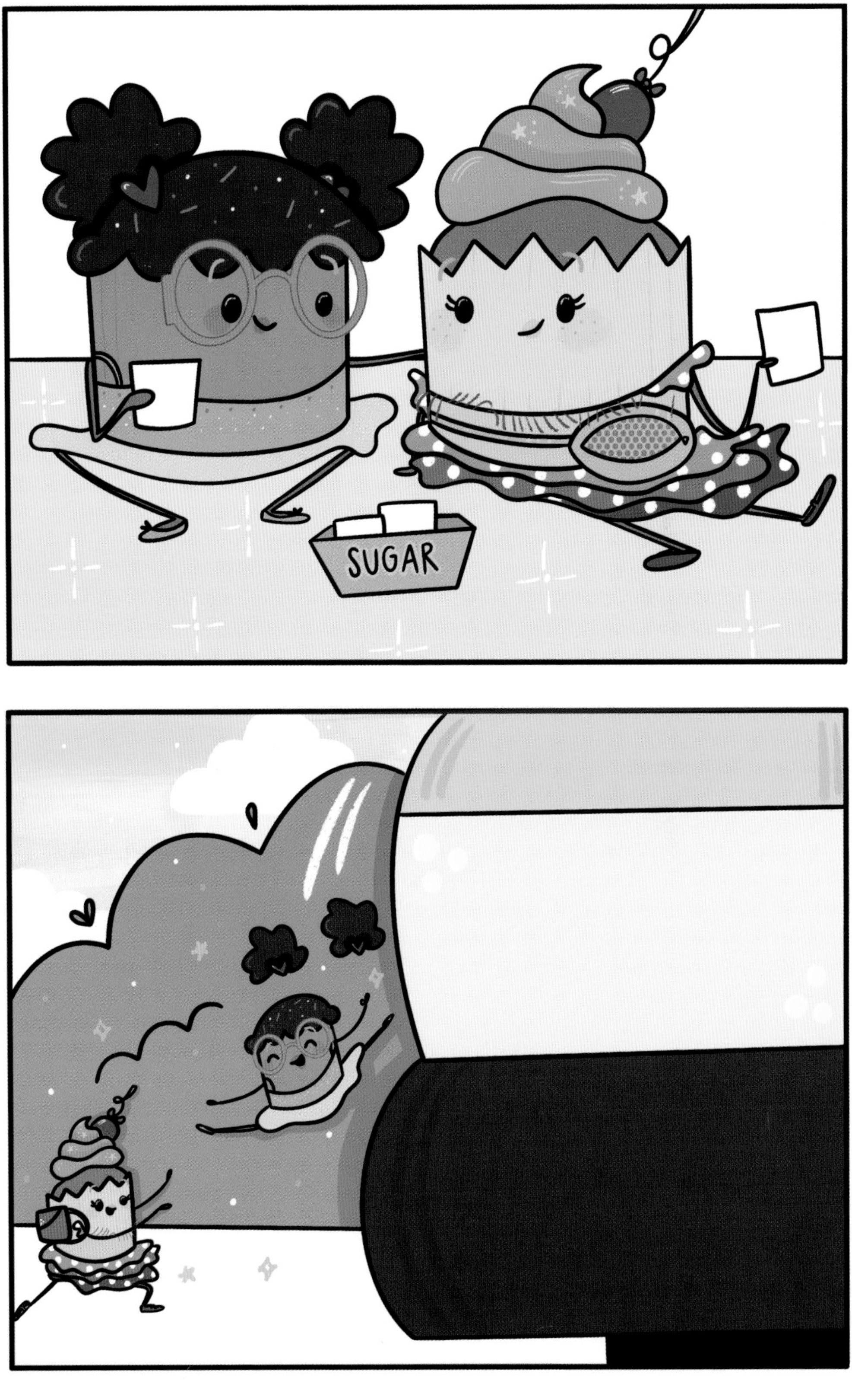
SUGAR

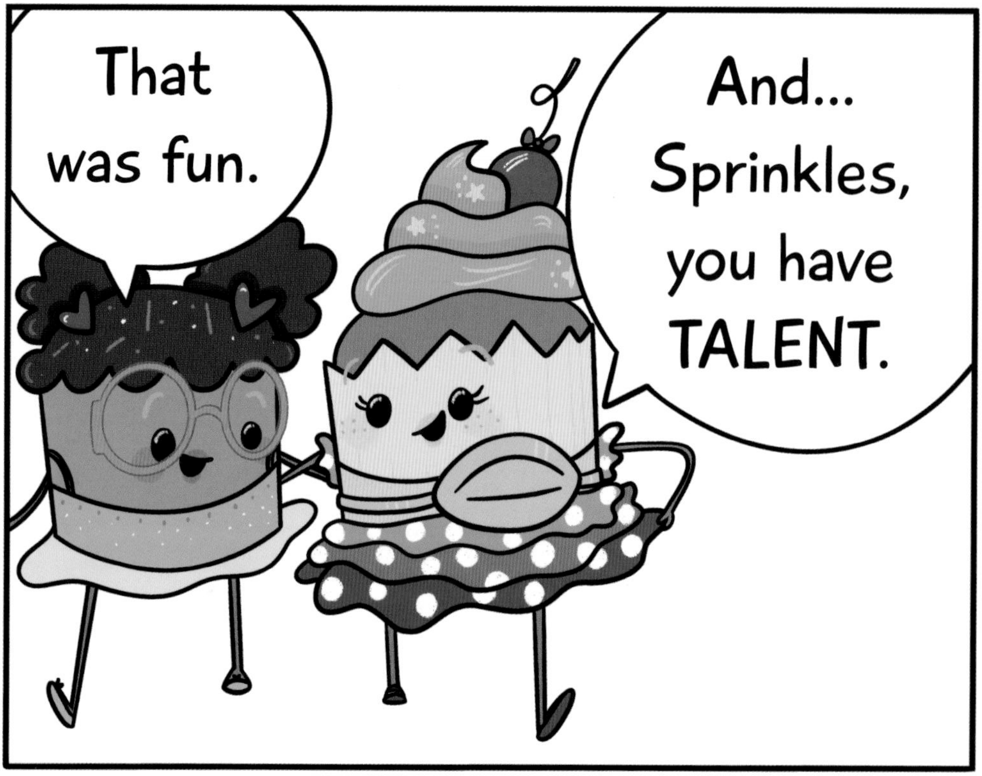
That was fun.
And... Sprinkles, you have TALENT.

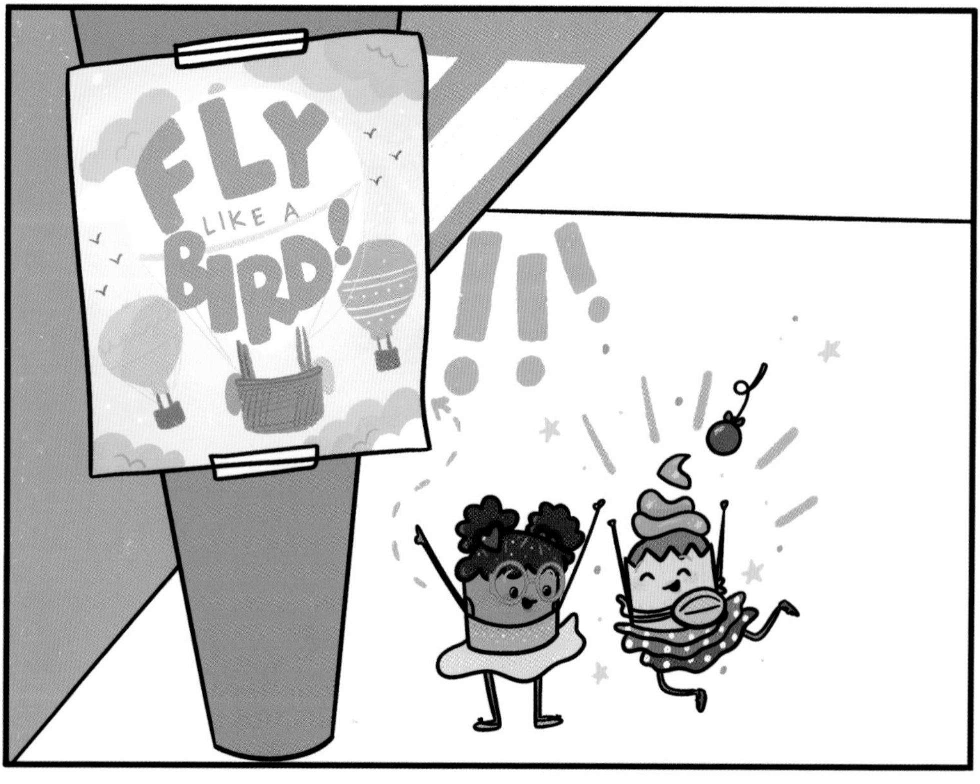
FLY LIKE A BIRD!
!!!

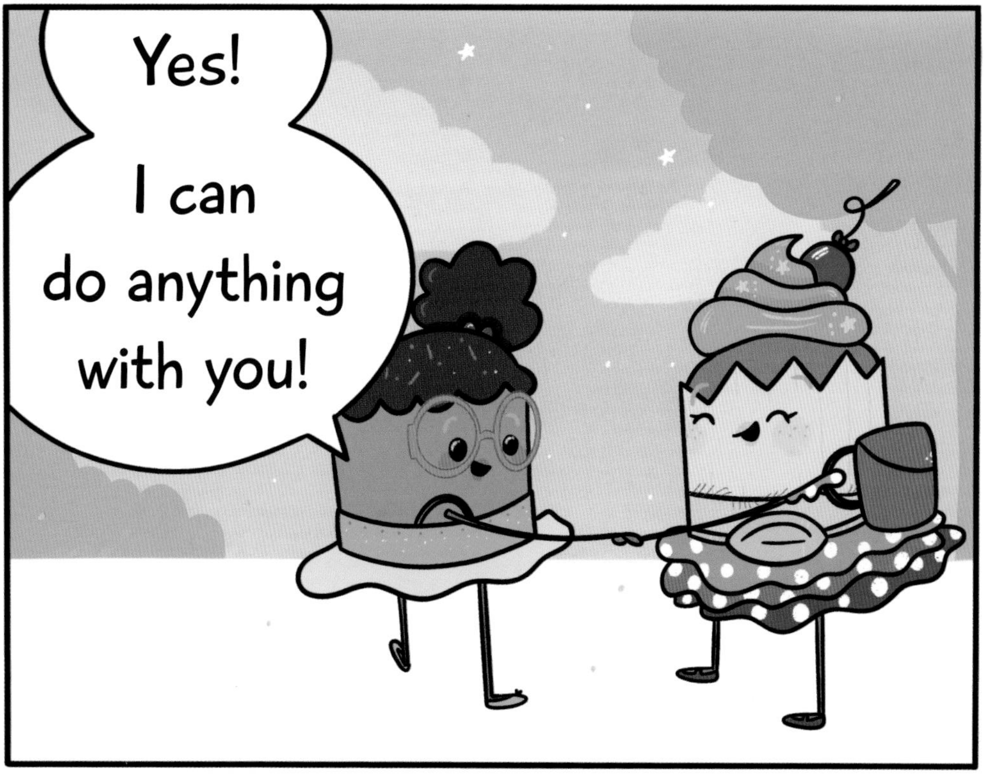
Yes!
I can do anything with you!

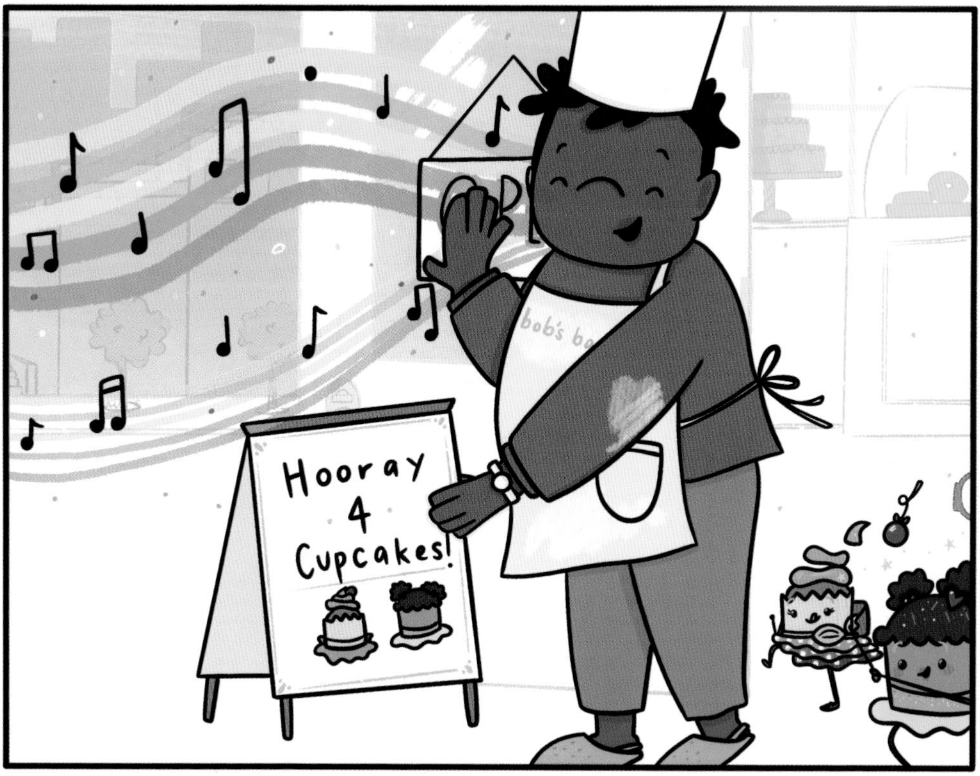
Hooray 4 Cupcakes!

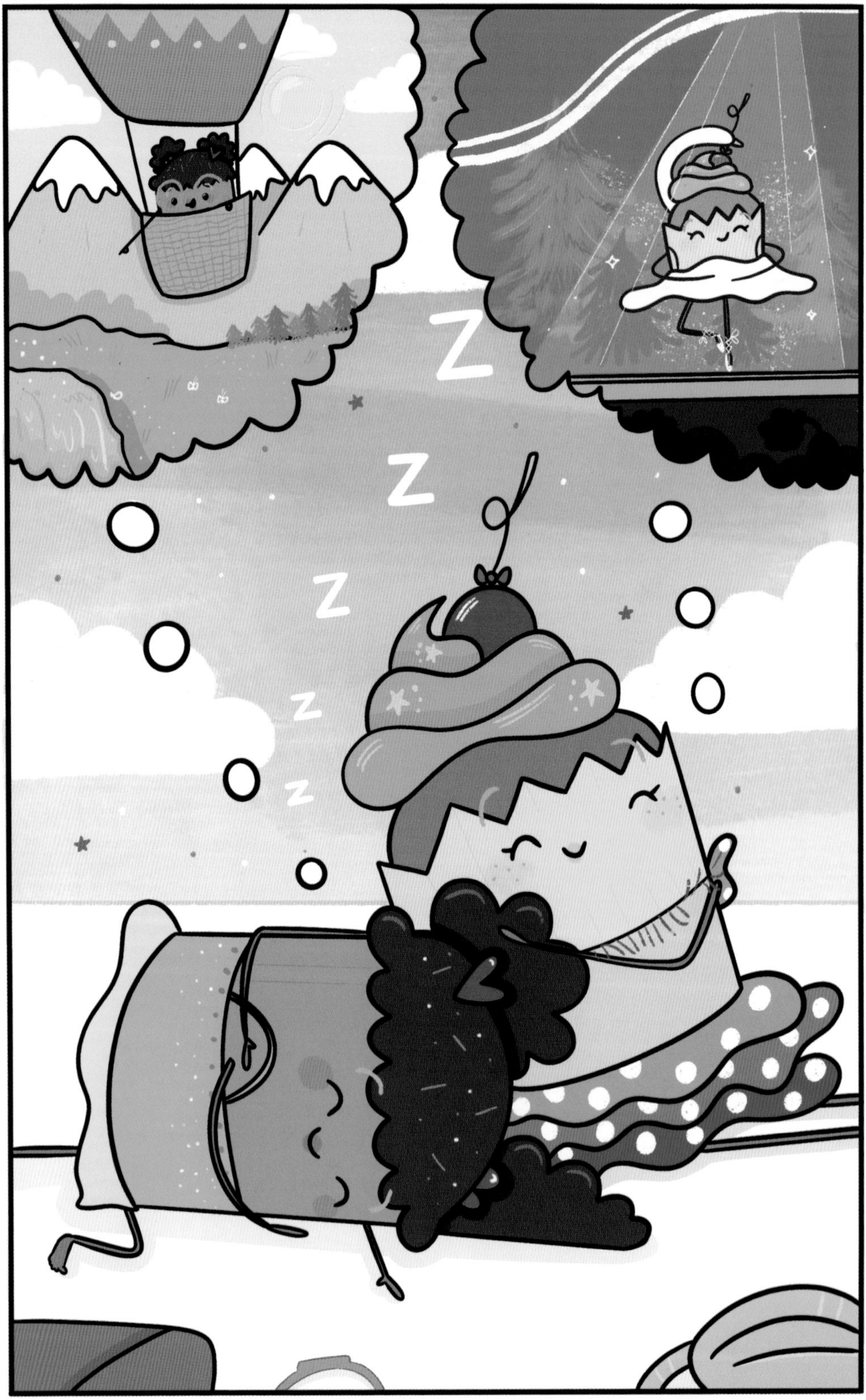
Z
Z
Z
Z
Z